Creighton's Crossroads

The Creighton Family Saga

Book One

by

Betty Larosa

AuthorHouse™
1663 Liberty Drive, Suite 200
Bloomington, IN 47403
www.authorhouse.com
Phone: 1-800-839-8640

© 2007 Betty Larosa. All rights reserved.

No part of this book may be reproduced, stored in a retrieval system, or transmitted by any means without the written permission of the author.

First published by AuthorHouse 12/19/2007

ISBN: 978-1-4343-3724-5 (sc)
ISBN: 978-1-4343-3723-8 (hc)

Library of Congress Control Number: 2007906764

Printed in the United States of America
Bloomington, Indiana

This book is printed on acid-free paper.

ACKNOWLEDGEMENTS

First and foremost, I must thank my husband Gene who has been with me throughout the entire process of writing this series of novels. From the first borrowed typewriter on the kitchen table, progressively through the IBM Selectric, the word processor, and now my latest computer, he has supported me, patiently answered my endless questions about all things military, and a man's point of view. I even purloined his copy of General U. S. Grant's *Memoirs* to do additional research for the last chapters of this book.

From here, the list is endless of those who showed support and encouragement. I want to thank Freda Bartlett, a friend and former co-worker, who read the very first horrible draft of my manuscript. Then my dear and valued neighbor Pat Orosz who proof read for me when I thought this book was ready for submission, and again at the end when it really was ready. My sister-in-law Becky Fresa had the misfortune of reading my next horrible draft as she recuperated from a skiing accident. My beautiful niece Britt Fresa didn't know what she was getting into when she agreed to read it later on. Her critiques and subsequent proof-reading leave me wanting for appropriate ways to express my gratitude.

Then I signed up for a writing class. That's when I met Gerald Swick who became my mentor, a general pain in the derriere, and constant friend. Only a friend would tell me what I needed to hear and he taught me a lot, not only about writing but about enduring. Thanks, Gerald. You were here at the right time and, thankfully, you still are. And I certainly cannot forget Charlie Hively whose advice was crisp and on the mark.

I am blessed to have another friend and mentor in Anna Smucker who agreed to critique the entire manuscript before it became a series. Words of praise and encouragement from an award-winning author and teacher are more than my efforts deserve, but her kind words kept me going. Saying thank you, Anna, doesn't seem like enough somehow.

That also applies to a friend, writer, and teacher, Belinda Anderson. Belinda taught me how to stretch the boundaries and gave sound advice at a workshop in the most gorgeous and inspiring setting deep in the mountains of West Virginia.

And then there is my critique group. A more unique, unlikely combination you will never find, but we supported one another, shared secrets, ghost stories, and even managed to critique each other's works. Through all that, we grew as friends and writers. How can I ever thank Kathy Curry for her steadfast belief in my project, or Hootie Blue Eyes for his remarkable insights? Many thanks go to Lenora Caldwell and Twyla Vincent. Each of you helped and supported me in your own distinctive way. I am grateful for your friendship.

Writing is not necessarily a solitary effort. Nor can it be accomplished without the feedback, the inquiries about progress, and words of encouragement from so many people. It's impossible to enumerate all those who helped sustain me when I felt like giving up. Thanks to all of you who did not let that happen. You know who you are.

Betty Larosa
Bridgeport, West Virginia

There is only one person to whom I can and do dedicate this novel: My soul mate, my best friend, and the love of my life.

> *"Never try to get revenge;*
> *Leave that, my friend, to God's anger."*
>
> St. Paul's letter to the Romans
> Chapter 12, verse 19

PHILIP
1858 – 1864

Chapter 1

THERE WAS NOTHING in the rising wind that held even a whiff of foreboding. Or possibilities.

But, on this brisk October evening, Philip Creighton was too distracted to notice. Thanks in no small measure to this most recent argument with his mother about his unexplained absences from those damned monthly socials she held for the chosen few of the town.

As he hurried down Main Street toward the Strand Hotel, his hands thrust into the pockets of his greatcoat, he decided that he definitely was not in the mood for this meeting with a New York businessman.

Lifting his face into the wind, Philip paused under the pool of light from a gas street lamp and gazed across the street at the bank established by his ancestor, the original Philip Creighton who had settled and developed the Susquehanna River valley town that now bears his name--Creighton's Crossroads. At the end of the block stood the yellow brick building occupied by the family-owned newspaper that still exerts considerable influence in the area.

Everywhere he looked, Philip could see evidence of his ancestors' civic involvement and ambition by forging their distinctive mark on this Pennsylvania community. He stood transfixed in the wash of the street lamp, struck suddenly by the realization that something was missing from his life. Here I am, he thought, twenty-six years old with nothing to show for my life so far. Nothing, except acting as caretaker to the Creighton holdings--still living with my parents, and fending off Mother's insistent meddling into my life.

He paused in his musings and shook his head. Damn it, he thought, this latest episode with Mother is forcing me to face several uncomfortable truths. It is long past time that I stop drifting along on the backs of my ancestors and strike out on my own. I am perfectly capable of making significant contributions to this community and building my personal legacy.

Then perhaps, I can rid myself of this great emptiness in my life.

With renewed energy and purpose, Philip now felt ready to face his business meeting, still unaware of portents swirling in the wind.

He entered the Strand Hotel lobby lit with gas chandeliers and an inviting fire that crackled in the huge fireplace. Pausing at the dining room door, he handed his greatcoat to an employee and surveyed the few diners inside.

The maitre d' greeted Philip with a bow. "Good evening, sir. Your table is ready."

"Thank you, Adolphus. I see there aren't many folks dining out this evening."

"Monday evenings are usually slow," Adolphus said. "This cold snap may have kept most people indoors. My mother predicts that we can expect snow flurries later tonight and she is usually correct about those things."

"Yes, she is," Philip chuckled. "Give your mother my best wishes."

"Yes, sir, I will. Thank you for remembering her."

Philip followed Adolphus to his table, smiling at the other diners as he strode by. Nearly six feet tall, broad-shouldered and trim, he boasted a full head of black curly hair, the hereditary mark of a Creighton. Those who had the misfortune of crossing him had seen his dark eyes flash fire, but he was, on the whole, even tempered and generous to the less fortunate.

"I am meeting a Mr. Ryder this evening. Please show him to my table when he arrives."

Slipping Adolphus a generous tip, he added, "I'll have some bourbon now to take the chill off, and a bottle of champagne from my private stock later on."

"Very good, sir."

Relaxing over his bourbon, Philip consulted his notes about this evening's meeting. He was scribbling a note to himself when he heard a soft feminine voice say, "Mr. Creighton?"

He jumped to his feet, nearly spilling his drink. "Yes, may I help you?" He smiled at the young lady in a dark green suit, clutching a fur muff. Her auburn hair, piled high on her head, was held in place by pearl hairpins. Green eyes regarded him evenly. Everything about her, he noted with appreciation, spoke of elegance and breeding.

She extended her hand. "My name is Samantha Ryder. I believe we have an appointment."

"You are S. A. Ryder?" he asked in an incredulous voice. Grinning sheepishly, he shook her hand. "Forgive me, I was expecting--"

"A man? Then I am sorry to disappoint you, sir."

"Oh no," he stammered. "Believe me, I am anything but disappointed. May I order you a drink?" He motioned to Adolphus for service.

Setting her muff aside, she took the seat Adolphus held for her. "Champagne, please."

"I have already taken the liberty of ordering." Snuffing out his cheroot in deference to her, several questions immediately popped into his mind. He asked the most obvious question first. "Was your husband unable to make the trip?"

"My husband is deceased," she replied in a strained voice.

The struggle for control of her emotions did not escape Philip's eye. "I'm sorry. How thoughtless of me."

She shook her head. "You had no way of knowing. It is I who beg your forgiveness, Mr. Creighton. I should have been more specific in my letter."

"There is nothing to forgive, Mrs. Ryder." With a gentle smile, he added, "We could go on like this all evening. This minor miscommunication is no one's fault. Ah, our champagne has arrived."

After Adolphus had poured for them, Philip exhaled a sigh of relief. "Well, shall we order?"

Only once during dinner did Philip's eyes stray from Samantha to a table where Arthur Stockton, a local businessman, was dining with a voluptuous young beauty. Her golden hair, swept up to set off her classic features, revealed ivory shoulders and a tantalizing neck. Her large hazel eyes were almost golden in the candlelight. My God, she is stunning, he marveled. With looks like that, she must be Stockton's mistress.

Samantha's questioning look brought Philip back to himself.

The meal passed pleasantly, with small talk and getting acquainted. Over coffee, the dreaded moment arrived when Philip knew they must address the reason for this meeting.

"Well," he said, leaning back in his chair, "after a delicious meal like that, I am in no mood to discuss business. Why don't we postpone this transaction to another time? Perhaps when our attorneys can be present." He started to rise.

"No, Mr. Creighton."

The firm resolve in her voice stopped him, and he sat down, puzzled.

Samantha continued in a determined tone, "I came all the way from New York to talk business with you and I intend to do just that." She rose from her seat and reached for her muff. "We can discuss the details in my suite. Have no fear, sir. You are in no danger of being seduced. My maid has accompanied me, so the proprieties will be observed."

Once they were settled in her suite, Samantha asked her maid Lucy to order coffee and brandy. As Philip observed the maid, he noted that she was a small-framed young girl, with mousy brown hair pulled into a tight bun. He could not determine the color of her eyes, for she kept them cast down in a subservient attitude to which his mother would have given her full approval as a servant knowing her place.

Shifting his attention to Samantha, he surveyed her soft curves, white skin and sweet smile. The inflection in her voice, however, warned him not to underestimate her resolve--or ability.

"So, Mr. Creighton," she turned to face him squarely, "shall we begin? I must warn you that my being a female does not mean that I am incapable of handling business matters. We women are fit for more than just keeping house and bearing children--as well as the abuses and tantrums of men. We are very well suited for other tasks, and in some instances, exceeding those of some men. My father is a Senator, a millionaire many times over. I grew up listening to business transactions at the dinner table." She fixed a challenging gaze on him. "Does dealing with a woman offend your male sensibilities?"

Philip considered for a moment before replying, "On the contrary. I consider myself a modern man. However, I must ask forbearance for the erroneous assumption that the S. A. Ryder who signed the letter requesting this meeting could only have been a man." With a wry smile, he added, "Believe me, Mrs. Ryder, I never for a moment questioned your capabilities."

Her gaze wavered. "I--I'm sorry for pre-judging you." She gave him a conciliatory smile. "I would prefer it if you called me Samantha."

"And you must call me Philip. Please." He indicated that she sit in the chair opposite him. "Now that we have the preliminaries out of the way, shall we get down to business?"

"First of all," she said once she was seated, "I am not willing to sell my timber lands."

Philip frowned. "Really? It is my understanding that an agreement exists between your husband and my agent to sell over three thousand acres, and that I'd operate the lumber mills."

"That was my late husband's agreement, not mine. Ready cash was all Alfred had on his mind. You see, he had invested poorly and accumulated huge gambling debts, which forced him to sell most of what he owned. My father tried to advise him but he was head-strong," her voice faltered, "especially when he had been drinking."

She leaned back and, resting against the back of the chair, began in a soft, faraway voice,

"Do you remember my telling you that my husband was deceased?"

"Yes."

"I killed him." She straightened up and regarded him without flinching. "Don't look so shocked, Philip. With sufficient provocation, even you could kill. Alfred and I had been married for nearly ten years. It had never been a happy marriage, merely an alliance of money and power.

"I learned early on that Alfred drank quite a bit. He also gambled and kept other women. I did not care what he did, so long as he left me alone. But he did not. When he drank, he became abusive. He would force his way into my room and beat me, then..." Pausing to control her emotions, she pressed a handkerchief to her lips.

Lucy entered at this point, discreetly placed a tray on the table, and left.

After the maid had closed the door, Philip encouraged her in a soft voice, "Take your time."

"I learned from my father that Alfred had been squandering my personal fortune to pay his gambling debts. He had even sold a diamond necklace my Grandmother VanderVoort had given me to pay his creditors. It took weeks for Father to track down the necklace and buy it back."

She exhaled a deep sigh. "After that, things grew worse. The beatings became more brutal. Sometimes, I could not go out for days because of the bruises on my face and body. I tried not to let Father see me in that condition.

"One night, Alfred was particularly desperate. He had borrowed a great deal of money from some disreputable men who demanded payment with exorbitant interest. He tried selling my timber acreage but Father had retained it in his name as a precaution against such a contingency. Alfred demanded that I forge Father's signature on the deed. When I refused, he beat me and even threatened to shoot me."

Philip grimaced at the images her remarks conjured up in his mind.

"Somehow, I managed to get away from him and run into the upstairs hall to call for help. He followed me. Struck me across the face with his gun. I--I'm not sure how it happened but when I raised my arms to defend myself, I must have swung at him. I heard a scream, then an awful thudding sound. At that point, I lost consciousness." Her voice crackled and faded.

Struggling to regain her composure, she continued, "Sometime later, when I regained my senses, I lifted my head and saw him lying at the bottom of the stairs, the gun still in his hand. Apparently, he had broken his neck in the fall. The servants helped me to my room and sent for Father. Lucy later told me that when Father saw the frightful condition I was in, he became so enraged that she feared for his heart."

Samantha sat up abruptly. "Talking about it now, it is as though it had happened to someone else." Her eyes hardened as she touched the brow above her left eye. "But the scar here reminds me that it did not happen to someone else."

"Were the police called in?" Philip asked, as he stole a glance at the thin white scar barely visible in her eyebrow.

"Yes. Father told them a thief had broken into the house, that Alfred heard my screams and tried to protect me. The police concluded that Alfred had been thrown down the stairs during his struggle with the intruder."

Turning toward Philip, her eyes searched his face. "I did not intend to kill him."

"Of course not." Philip offered his hand in support. "You were only defending yourself."

He sat back and stared into the fireplace for a moment. "It appears we have a dilemma. I came here tonight with every intention of making you a fair offer on your property. Now, having heard your reasons for not wanting to sell, I fully understand your position and would like to offer my services in any way I can. Perhaps help you find a manager for your properties."

She gave him a tearful smile. "How kind of you, Philip. I do need help just now. I have relied on my father too much."

"It is settled then," he said in his take-charge voice, and rose from his seat. "Tomorrow, you will return to New York. I will follow in a day or so, after I have cleared up a few pending items here. Well, now that we have decided on a course of action, I think it is time I took my leave."

Samantha followed him to the shadowy foyer. Handing him his greatcoat and gloves, she said, "Thank you again, Philip, for being so kind. And for listening."

"You are a valiant lady, my dear. I will come for you at eleven o'clock tomorrow morning and escort you to the train station. Good night." He bowed and left her.

Descending the main staircase to the lobby, he couldn't help wondering at the disquieting effect this lovely stranger had had on him. When he stepped outside onto the plank sidewalk, he was greeted by snow flakes swirling in the biting wind. So, he thought with a smile,

Adolphus' mother had been correct in her prediction about snow flurries this evening.

Over the next four months, Philip's visits to New York increased. He soon became aware that his feelings for Samantha had intensified with each trip. Together, they had interviewed applicants, socialized and, on several occasions, enjoyed dinners with her father, Senator Tate. But by mid-February of 1859, they'd found no suitable manager from among the few applicants.

On the last evening of this particular visit, Philip and Samantha enjoyed a farewell dinner in the glittering atmosphere of Delmonico's. Over coffee, Philip leaned close to her and said, "I hate to leave, but I have stayed away from my own affairs too long. Believe me when I say that I am reluctant to leave such lovely company."

"Why, Mr. Creighton, you will turn my head with remarks like that."

He clasped her hand and whispered, "I mean it, Samantha. I have thought of nothing but you since we met. I even dared to hope that I might call on you."

"I rather hoped you would."

"I will keep in touch with you by mail, and as soon as I can manage it, I will return." His eyes twinkled with mischief. "To tend to business, of course."

"Of course," she said with a smile, and returned the pressure of his fingers.

When they came out of the restaurant, they were delighted to find that a light snow had fallen and lay sparkling under the gas lamps, giving the city a fairy tale appearance.

Philip hailed a cab and once they were snuggled down under the lap robe, he took her in his arms. "You don't know how much I hate leaving," he whispered, and kissed her for the first time. "Oh, my dear Samantha, how can I stay away from you?"

"You must not stay away," she answered, and returned his kiss with equal ardor.

After a cab ride that seemed all too short, Philip escorted her to the door. Kissing her hand, he promised to return as soon as possible.

Back inside the cab, Philip felt his pulse pounding. Had a simple misunderstanding over a business letter turned my life around? Can Samantha fill this void in my life?

God, I hope so.

Chapter 2

BY MID-MARCH, PHILIP was frustrated about being unable to find a suitable manager for Samantha's timber property. His parents, Ursula and Henry, and sister, Jessica, exchanged puzzled glances across the dinner table.

"The applicants," Philip continued, "are either unwilling to move to the Maine wilderness with their families, or we cannot agree on a salary. I was about to give up hope when an obvious solution came to mind. I plan to present my idea when Samantha and I meet again this week to review the latest prospects."

"Would you mind sharing this idea with me?" Henry asked, giving Philip his full attention.

"Of course, Pa. Perhaps you can determine if it has merit. As I stated, the reason applicants will not accept the job is always the same-- location and money. So, I concluded, why not eliminate these objections by offering a cottage with expenses in addition to the salary?"

"An excellent solution," Henry smiled. "Finding good managers is difficult. When you do find one, keep him happy and you'll earn his loyalty as well. That is the key to a smooth running operation."

Philip exhaled a sigh of relief. "Thanks for your support, Pa. As you are leaving town on Wednesday, I am unable to go to New York, so I asked Samantha to come here." Turning to Ursula, he said, "I invited Samantha to have dinner with us on Thursday. I would like the family to meet her. I hope you don't mind, Mother."

"Of course not, dear," Ursula assured him in a sugary voice. "Thursday will be just fine."

At two minutes past seven o'clock, Samantha arrived at the Creighton home in Philip's carriage. Shrugging off her ermine-trimmed velvet cape, she cut a regal figure in her royal blue evening dress. On her ears sparkled sapphire and diamond ear bobs.

Still awed by her beauty, Philip whispered, "Welcome to our home, my dear."

"Thank you, Philip," she murmured, and handed her gloves and cape to the maid.

Jessica appeared at that moment with a shy smile. The youngest of the four siblings, with her dark eyes and curly black hair, she was a true Creighton, and had blossomed into a pretty fifteen-year old.

"Jessica," Philip was saying, "allow me to present Mrs. Ryder. Samantha, this is my sister, Jessica."

Samantha gave her a warm smile. "Good evening, Jessica. You are even lovelier than Philip described."

Jessica curtsied in a becoming manner. "Thank you, Mrs. Ryder. I am happy to meet you."

Philip offered his arm to Samantha. "Shall we go into the parlor so I can introduce you to Mother?" He escorted the ladies into the parlor, resplendent with its gilt pier mirrors and dark, ponderous furniture.

Ursula was seated in her chair, queen-like, as one receiving lesser mortals into her presence. Dressed in a dove-gray silk evening dress, a diamond brooch glittering at her throat, she was a handsome woman. Her dark hair, streaked with gray at the temples, accentuated her clear, unlined complexion. Her pale blue eyes were glacial. And intimidating.

Struck by her imposing presence, Philip decided at that moment that she could have been a beautiful woman, but she lacked some necessary element. What was it? A soul, perhaps?

"Mother," he said, suppressing the mental question, "I have the honor to present Samantha Ryder. My dear, this is my mother, Ursula."

Smiling graciously, Ursula extended her hand. "Welcome to our home, Mrs. Ryder."

Samantha shook Ursula's hand. "Good evening, Mrs. Creighton. It is a pleasure to meet you at last. And please, call me Samantha."

"May I offer you a sherry before dinner, my dear?" Ursula motioned for the maid to pour.

"I am afraid there will be just the four of us this evening. Mr. Creighton is out of town on business and begs to be excused."

Philip hastened to add, "Pa did, however, express the desire to meet you very soon."

"I look forward to making his acquaintance."

Ursula waved her lace handkerchief in a gesture of resignation. "Ah, well, being a Creighton does have its demands on one's time. Our eldest son, George, also sends his regrets. His wife, Ellen, is indisposed, so naturally he is hesitant about leaving her. Her condition sometimes causes her--to feel unwell, or to swoon."

Samantha took a seat on the sofa opposite Ursula and said with concern, "Oh dear, I do hope it is nothing serious."

Philip twitched his lips to suppress a smile. "They are expecting," he whispered.

Samantha smiled at him, then at Ursula. "How wonderful for them."

Ursula shot Philip a sharp glance. Pursing her lips in disapproval, she added, "I find it difficult to speak of such things in mixed company."

Ignoring her rebuke, as he usually did, Philip said to Samantha, "I have a younger brother, Matthew, who is away at school."

"Yes," Ursula said with a smile. "Matthew is studying law at the University of Virginia. And, of course, you have met our Jessie," she reached for Jessica's hand, "who will break many hearts, I am sure, before she marries."

Samantha started to agree just as the maid entered to announce that dinner was served.

During dinner, Philip fussed over Samantha. She responded by patting his hand and chiding him gently, "Philip, you must not concern yourself about me. I'm fine."

"I just want to make sure you are comfortable."

She squeezed his hand. "I am quite comfortable, thank you."

Ursula raised an eyebrow at their meaningful glances and hand-holding. "My dear, you must tell us something about yourself," she said, showing only smiling interest. "Your family and where you attended school."

"Unfortunately, I have no brothers or sisters. It is just my father and me since Mother passed on twelve years ago."

Ursula offered the obligatory condolences.

"You might find this of interest, Mother," Philip interjected. "Samantha's maternal Dutch ancestors have been in New York since it was called New Amsterdam."

"Really?" Ursula said, giving her an appraising look. "You must be proud of your ancestry. Did you attend private schools, dear?"

"Yes, and later, I went abroad to study art history at the Sorbonne in Paris."

"How exciting," Jessica cooed. "Paris must be lovely. And so romantic."

"I really could not say," Samantha replied, shaking her head. "I was so homesick that I begged Father to let me return home."

"How unfortunate," Ursula said. "Although, I imagine your father was happy to have you with him again." She took a sip of wine before adding, "I understand you had been married. Are you divorced?"

"Mother, really," Philip protested with a frown.

Samantha placed a restraining hand on his arm. To Ursula, she replied, "No, I am not divorced. My husband died well over a year ago. Besides, my religion frowns on divorce."

Ursula gripped the stem of her wineglass. "Your religion?" she asked with raised eyebrows.

Before Philip could intervene, Samantha answered, "Yes, the Catholic Church forbids divorce. I believe several other religions do as well." Placing her fork beside her dessert dish, she looked at Philip with pleading eyes.

Philip shot Ursula a meaningful glare. "Mother, perhaps Samantha and Jessie would like to discuss something else."

"Yes, of course," Ursula agreed, and flashed her best hostess smile. "Shall we repair to the parlor for coffee?"

Later, inside Philip's closed carriage, Samantha leaned against Philip's shoulder and cried, "Oh, Philip, your mother hates me."

"You mustn't think such things." He slipped his arm around her. "Besides, it doesn't matter what Mother thinks. Knowing her obsession with illustrious lineages," he added with a cocked eyebrow, "I made sure she knew that your ancestors go back even farther than the Creightons' by at least one hundred years. You see, I cannot resist having fun at her expense."

He gave her a tender kiss. "My dear, I would never let anything or anyone stand in the way of our happiness. Not even Mother. Besides, why shouldn't she like you? You have an excellent background, impeccable breeding and a good family name."

"Like a prize thoroughbred," Samantha answered with a tinge of bitterness.

"Samantha, I am surprised at you. Don't you know how important you are to me? My only thought is to make you happy."

"You do make me happy, Philip." She caressed his face. "Happier than I ever dreamed possible."

"Perhaps you need more convincing evidence of my deep affection for you." He kissed her again, possessively, passionately.

"Philip, please," she protested, after catching her breath, "what if someone sees us?"

"I don't care." Tightening his embrace, he whispered against her cheek, "I love you, Samantha. I cannot wait much longer for you. We must talk about our future." He leaned back against the carriage seat, breathless and trembling. "To tell the truth, I see no point to a long, drawn out courtship."

"Oh, Philip, I do love you. I have never said that to any man."

He kissed her again, this time almost devouring her.

Philip returned home more than an hour later, slightly disheveled, and smiling. Ursula's shadowy figure in the upstairs hall jolted him back to reality.

Blocking access to his bedroom, Ursula stood firm, her arms crossed over her ample bosom. "So, you have finally torn yourself away from her."

Still smiling, he stood in the wash of the gaslight with the look of love upon him. "Yes, and it was difficult. I trust you are as taken with Samantha as I am," he said as he shouldered his way past her into his room.

Ursula followed him. "I assure you, my feelings about Samantha are as strong as yours."

"Somehow, that does not reassure me." He spun around to face her squarely, his eyes now flashing fire. "I must say that I found your questions at dinner atrocious and insulting."

She regarded him warily before asking "How far have things gone between you? Are you thinking in terms of the future?"

"Those are my plans."

"Have you taken several important issues into consideration?"

Philip untied his cravat with an impatient jerk. "Such as?"

"Her prior marriage aside, Mrs. Ryder engages in commerce, which I would attribute to her Dutch ancestry that seems to have impressed you so. Personally, I find that an unladylike quality. And, there is the matter of her religion."

He gave her a chilling smile. "Now we are at the heart of the matter, aren't we? I would ask you to remember that Samantha is a widow, and an honorable lady. As for her religion," he shrugged, "it presents no problem for me."

Ursula's eyes widened. "May I remind you of who you are? While I am certain Mrs. Ryder may be honorable, she has been married before. I think you deserve better than that."

"Are you insinuating...?" he sputtered, unable to finish the question.

"Please, dear," she reasoned in her overly-calm, Mother-in-charge voice, "I am merely pointing out several conspicuous issues. Think for a moment. Are you sure she is the woman for you?"

Philip glowered at her. "Samantha possesses intelligence, grace and beauty. She more than exceeds my expectations. How can you possibly object to that?"

"That is all well and good, but you know how this family feels about anything that smacks of popery. I cannot imagine what your Grandfather Jasper would say if he were here."

Philip felt hot rage rise within him. "Despite what you--or Grandpa Jasper--may think, I am perfectly capable of making a mature decision about the woman I choose to marry. In the meantime, I must ask you to be polite to Samantha."

Ursula drew herself up in response to his implication. "I am polite to all my guests. You need not imply otherwise. And you need not shout."

He lowered his voice but his tone remained icy. "Your insinuations about Samantha are so infuriating that I find it difficult not to shout."

"I hope you'll do nothing to dishonor your father's name, or bring shame upon this family."

"I have never, nor do I ever intend to disgrace the venerable Creighton name. As a matter of fact, you will have the opportunity to prove your sincerity about being gracious to Samantha. I have invited her to have tea with you tomorrow." A challenging look played about his eyes.

"In that case," Ursula said, matching his look, "I shall be as gracious to the lady as she deserves."

Chapter 3

THE NEXT DAY, Ursula stood at the top of the stairs, her heart racing in anticipation of Samantha's arrival. She was dressed in her finest dusty rose afternoon dress with delicate ivory lace at the neck and wrists, and a four-strand pearl choker at her throat, a gift from Henry to assuage one of her famous piques. In her most imperious manner, she surveyed her domain.

The current Creighton family home, built in 1810 by her late father-in-law, the indomitable Jasper Creighton, sits adjacent to the site of the original Philip's log homestead. The Creighton family history, however, harkens back to the mid-1750s when the first Philip Creighton, second son of a prosperous Liverpool merchant, left home and hearth in England to make his own way in the new world.

The ambitious nineteen year old Philip landed in Baltimore harbor where he worked at menial jobs for his keep. He subsequently met and married seventeen year old Hannah Hawkins, the daughter of a former neighbor in Liverpool. Like so many émigrés before them, the young couple moved westward to begin their new life. They settled in the fertile Susquehanna River valley where he purchased a tract of land.

Discovering early on that he'd rather work with his brain than with his hands, Philip sold his tract for a tidy profit and bought more land. Prospering through his business acumen, he began lending money to new settlers, became the local notary and, ultimately, the banker. It seemed inevitable that he would become the publisher of the town's first newspaper, thereby influencing local politics. He exercised this influence by arranging for the passenger and mail stagecoaches to pass through the burgeoning crossroads.

Each subsequent generation carried on the family businesses that grew into a minor empire. As the fortune grew, so did the ambition of the Creightons until Jasper Creighton, grandson of the original Philip, decided he needed a more suitable home for his family, something befitting his social and financial status.

This handsome brick mansion, where Ursula now holds court, boasts 14 rooms, seven-foot high windows, four interior chimneys and a Palladian-style entry. Henry had grown up in this house, along with his older brother, Benjamin Philip. Their mother, Clara, had initiated the tradition of inviting the townspeople into the home on the first Sunday of each month to enjoy refreshments and pleasant society.

Thanks to my loyalty to family values, Ursula thought, as she descended the wide staircase, that tradition continues to this day. Crossroads society may not be as grand as New York's but we do maintain certain standards. And it is the Creightons who set those standards. When Mrs. Ryder leaves here this afternoon, she will harbor no illusions about Philip's intentions.

And some day, Philip will thank me for protecting his interests.

She inspected the formal parlor in her meticulous manner before instructing the maid, "You may serve us in here, Jenny, and be sure to use the silver tea service. We must put our best foot forward for Mrs. Ryder."

"Yes, ma'am," Jenny replied with a respectful curtsy.

Promptly at four o'clock, the brass knocker sounded on the front door. Ursula's heart leapt. Consulting the pier mirror in the parlor for one last check of her appearance, she was shocked to see that anticipation of the coming event had made her color shockingly high. She had barely composed herself when the maid announced her guest.

Samantha swept into the parlor, all regal bearing and composure, wearing a green wool cape with sable trim over a matching suit. Her manner, the assurance in her voice, all spoke of money and breeding. With her soft aura of maturity, Ursula realized with trepidation that this was no sweet young maiden who can be easily manipulated.

"Samantha, dear," Ursula said with a smile. "My, don't you look pretty in green. It does so much to compliment your lovely eyes."

"Thank you, Mrs. Creighton," Samantha murmured with a smile as she handed her cape to the maid.

Ursula invited Samantha to be seated, indicating the most uncomfortable chair in the room. To the maid, she said, "Jenny, please bring the tea in directly."

Jenny nodded and hurried away.

"So," Ursula began, as they settled down in the stiff, forbidding room, "are you having a pleasant stay in Creighton's Crossroads? I do hope you do not find it too provincial, compared to New York."

"On the contrary," Samantha said. "My accommodations at the Strand are comfortable, and Philip is attentive to my every need. This morning, we accomplished what we both believed impossible. We finally hired a manager for my Maine timber properties. I am so relieved and grateful to Philip for his assistance."

Ursula's heart constricted with jealousy at that glowing young face so full of love for her favorite son. Suppressing a twinge of conscience, she plunged ahead. "I recall your telling me that you are an only child."

"Yes." Samantha lowered her eyes. "You must forgive me if I confess to more than a little envy of your lovely family."

"Thank you, my dear. The Creightons have always taken great pride in their family and their traditions." Ursula reached across the small space between the sofa and the chair where Samantha sat and patted her hand. "Philip is usually reticent about mentioning it, but he was named after the founding father of Creighton's Crossroads. It is a tradition carried on by each generation."

Feeling at ease in her setting, Ursula took consolation in the hovering presence she suddenly felt of every Creighton who had lived before her. Peering over her shoulder. Listening to her every utterance. Whispering and nodding their approval of her intentions this day.

"Ah, here is our tea," Ursula said, as Jenny entered, bearing a tray. "Thank you, Jenny. I will pour. Do you take sugar and cream, Samantha?"

"No, thank you. Just lemon."

"I do enjoy my tea. Earl Grey, of course. My only vice, if you don't mind my saying so." Ursula gave her a conspiratorial smile as though sharing a naughty secret. "Now, we were speaking of your family. I was sorry to learn of your husband's passing."

"You are very kind, ma'am," Samantha answered in a calm voice as she accepted the cup from her hostess.

The quiver of her guest's hand and the slight hesitation in her voice did not escape Ursula's notice.

Drawing in a deep breath, Samantha went on with a forced smile, "I cannot believe I have been seeing Philip since October. These last six months have flown by."

"My, my," Ursula clucked into her teacup, "has it been that long?"

"I imagine Philip has told you about his plans. Our plans," Samantha corrected with a shy smile.

"Plans?" Ursula asked, looking shocked, and quite innocent. "He has not spoken to me of any plans. Whatever can you mean?"

"Surely he must have mentioned something by now." Wide-eyed, Samantha pressed her napkin to her lips. "Oh, good heavens, I cannot have violated his confidence."

Ursula shook her head in bewilderment. "Forgive me for saying so, but you speak as if Philip actually intends to marry you."

"He gave me that impression," Samantha answered in a strangled voice. "That is why he brought me here, isn't it? To meet his family?" Staring in astonishment, she searched Ursula's eyes for some sign of confirmation.

"My dear," Ursula cooed, all sweetness and concern, "you must appreciate Philip's position in this community. However, I feel certain that he will be discreet in his arrangements with you. Where he will situate you. Things of that nature."

The color drained from Samantha's face. "What are you saying?"

"Oh, come now, Samantha, we both understand what is expected. You are a mature woman, willing to give Philip what he wants. But marriage," Ursula laughed a brittle, insinuating laugh, "surely you don't think..."

She watched as Samantha placed her cup on the tray with quivering hands. Waited as the poor stunned woman stood unsteadily and reached for her cape and gloves.

"Thank you for your hospitality, Mrs. Creighton," Samantha said in a quavering voice. "I really must leave now."

Ursula likewise rose from her seat. "Oh, must you leave so soon? I pray you will visit us again before you return to New York."

"I--I'm afraid not. I really must go," Samantha repeated in a hoarse whisper. She shook Ursula's hand and swept from the room, her eyes misted with tears.

Long after Jenny had closed the front door behind Samantha, Ursula stood on the threshold of the parlor's double doors with her hands clasped sedately, her smile triumphant.

"Humph," she said aloud to the empty room, "I expected more from the girl than that. It was so effortless it was hardly any fun at all."

Chapter 4

SAMANTHA'S TRAIN HAD already left the station, its mournful whistle sounding in the distance, when her note was delivered to Philip's office. Through misty eyes, he read the words that changed his life, and his outlook, forever.

"My dearest Philip,
Yes, Philip, you are very dear to me, but it has become clear that my expectations for our future and yours are worlds apart. Please forgive me, but I cannot share that kind of future with you. I am truly grateful for your help in setting my business affairs in order. It would be to no one's advantage to see each other again. I leave you, disappointed, but with fondest regards.
                                                            Samantha"

Philip set the note aside, stood by his office window and stared out at the bleak March afternoon. What did she mean about our expectations being far apart? What was the future she envisioned? Has she changed her mind about marrying me? I'll write to her, ask her to explain what she means. No, I'll go to New York, see her face to face, and force her to tell me what happened. I must do something. I cannot lose her. I must...

Picking up the note again, his eyes fell on the sentence about not contacting her and his heart sank. Swallowing the bitterness rising in his throat, he tossed the note onto his desk. What good would it do to write to her? As she pointed out, there is no advantage to it. She has obviously changed her mind about spending her life with me.

He slumped into his chair with his chin on his chest, recalling that she'd seemed as eager for marriage as he, and reciprocated his love with warmth and openness. She had even declared her love for him. What changed her mind?

Filled with sudden determination, he sat up and slammed his fist against the arm of his chair. Well, by God, I am going to find out. Why should I sit around wondering?

After dinner that evening, Philip went straight to his room. Seated at his writing table, he wrote a letter to Samantha, asking specific questions about why she left him: Have I done something? Have I not done something? What could have changed your mind so abruptly? I must have answers. Tell me, please.

Next morning, Ursula spied the envelope addressed to Samantha on the entry hall table.

"Jenny, what is this?" she asked the maid, holding up the envelope.

"Mr. Philip asked me to give it to the postman this morning, ma'am," she replied with innocent candor.

Ursula pursed her lips. "In that case, I had better put my own correspondence out so the postman can take them too." She hurried away to the morning room with firm purpose.

When Jennie handed the letters to the postman later that morning, with her usual giggle and wink, one envelope was missing from the stack of outgoing mail.

* * *

For weeks afterward, no one dared to mention Samantha's abrupt departure to Philip.

Usually kind and attentive, he was distracted, forbidding any word of consolation. In his dealings with the public, or at his office, he had to be brought back to the moment. During meals at home, his family glanced at each other as Philip toyed with his food, or wandered away from the conversation at social gatherings.

But no one dared speak of it.

Seeing the pain Samantha's departure was causing him, Ursula wondered if her actions had been too harsh. Then, realizing the consequences if she had not taken such drastic measures, she felt confident that she had taken the proper course. Philip's future, as well as the Creighton name, must be considered. Old Jasper himself would rise up out of his mausoleum if Philip allied himself with a Catholic, she concluded with a jerk of her chin. The purity of the family dynasty must be preserved.

Philip wandered aimlessly through his daily routine as he awaited Samantha's reply. He hurried home each evening to check the mail. He also valued the understanding silence his family accorded him during this agonizing time.

He did, however, think it odd that Ursula, who characteristically voiced an opinion on everything, had not made one of her judgmental pronouncements on this particular issue. He wondered if she might be aware of the reason for Samantha's sudden change of heart. After all, he reasoned, they'd had tea together that day.

Guilt, uncertainty, anger, all the elements that destroy a man's self-esteem, continued to hound Philip for weeks afterward. But he received no reply from Samantha.

Philip had just approved a loan application when the door to his office opened. His assistant Tom Dayton stood in the doorway to announce a visitor when Ursula brushed past him saying, "Thank you, Mr. Dayton. I will announce myself."

Philip stood with a half-smile. "This is a surprise. What can I do for you, Mother?"

"Hello, Philip, dear. I wanted to show off my new hat that just arrived from Philadelphia. What do you think?" She turned slowly, affording him a view from all angles.

"Quite becoming," he observed without enthusiasm.

"I am feeling festive today, so I thought perhaps you would like to escort me to luncheon."

"If you wish. Just give me a moment to finish this paperwork."

Seated in the Strand Hotel dining room twenty minutes later, Ursula broke the awkward silence by asking in a concerned, motherly voice, "How are you feeling, dear?"

"Fine." He frowned then threw down his napkin. "No, I'm not fine. I've re-read Samantha's note, but I still cannot make sense of it. Would you please read it and tell me what you think?"

"Oh, dear," she said, as she accepted the folded paper and held it before her as though it were on fire, "I am hesitant to intrude into such personal matters. However, if it is your wish..." After placing her spectacles on her nose, she read the note carefully before commenting. "How extraordinary. It is so mysterious. Whatever can it mean?"

"I have no idea," he replied, retrieving the note. "Did you observe anything out of the ordinary when you had tea with her? Did she seem distracted or upset? Or say anything at all?"

Ursula patted his hand. "I have already studied on it, dear, but can recall nothing that seemed amiss. I found her a most pleasant companion, intelligent and, I must admit, quite lovely."

Philip lowered his eyes, remembering exactly how lovely and companionable she was.

"While I can overlook the fact that she had been married before--" Ursula began.

"Widowed," Philip corrected tersely.

"I'm sorry--widowed. Nonetheless, we cannot disregard the other matter."

Philip rolled his eyes in disgust. "Yes, I know. You have made yourself abundantly clear on the subject of her religion."

"Other than that," Ursula sighed, "I believe she would have made an excellent wife for you."

Philip rested his elbows on the table and leaned closer, suspicion growing within him. "She gave no indication of what she was thinking or feeling when she left you?"

Ursula appeared to give his question careful consideration. "No, none. There is one thing I hesitate to mention, dear. Have you considered that she may have sensed something that would have presented a problem later on?"

Philip's head came up sharply. "You mean her religion?"

"I am merely offering a possibility. Whatever it may have been, Samantha obviously felt it serious enough to end this thing between you, quickly and cleanly. I suppose it is more merciful that way," she added with deep concern.

Philip leaned back in his chair and stared at her, wide-eyed. "Merciful? What is merciful about leaving me with no explanation?"

"Please, son," she patted his hand, "you must not torture yourself like this. I am certain you did nothing to bring this about, so you must not consume yourself with doubts or recriminations. I am confident that whatever happened, you are not to blame."

Having allayed the nagging feeling that Ursula may have known something, Philip threw himself into his work even more to occupy his tortured mind. Somehow, he reminded himself repeatedly, I must forget the kisses we shared. Or how she felt in my arms.

Oh God, he groaned deep within himself, I must drive all those things from my mind or go mad from remembering.

Spring moved into the summer of 1859, and Philip gradually became more involved in the family gatherings. He did, however, continue to absent himself from his mother's monthly socials to avoid the posturing and twittering of the local young maidens. His only respite on those afternoons was the secret poker games with his three closest friends, Denton Cobb, Robert Strickland, and Leland Myles.

During the family's month-long July vacation at Cape Island, New Jersey, Philip could be seen early each morning, strolling alone on the beach. Walking barefoot through the surf with his head down and his hands jammed into his pockets, he seemed oblivious to the gulls wheeling and screeching overhead. Or the curious stares from other vacationers.

Chapter 5

WITH THE ONSET of autumn and winter, the Crossroads social season began. One of the major events of the season was the coming out party of Miss Elizabeth Stockton.

On the evening of the gala affair, music floated on the crisp December air. The windows of the Stockton home blazed with candles. Furniture was pushed against the walls in the dining room and parlor to make room for dancing. Laughing young people exchanged dance cards, and flirted at the punch bowl.

The Creighton family persuaded Philip at last that it was time he resumed his social life so, with great reluctance, he agreed to accompany them to the party. To his amazement, he found that he was enjoying himself. He joked with the other eligible bachelors while eyeing the available belles as they waltzed by in the arms of their partners. The entire room seemed to sway with music, hoop skirts and faces flushed with excitement.

Miss Elizabeth Stockton, the center of attention, was a vision of loveliness in her white satin ball gown, replete with bows, ruffles and wide hoops. She wore her golden hair in the latest style, entwined with pearls and small garlands of flowers, showing off her neck and alabaster shoulders to great advantage. Her large hazel eyes sparkled in the glow of the candles, revealing soft yellow flecks when she smiled.

Philip stood beside the punch bowl with Denton Cobb, his long time friend and personal attorney whose office was the location of their secret Sunday afternoon poker games. Compared to Philip's dark good looks and forceful presence, Denton was thin, pale and bookish, with light brown hair and wire-rimmed glasses. Despite their differences in appearance and temperament, Denton and Philip had shared confidences and pranks since their school days, along with their other friends and poker-playing buddies, Leland and Robert.

Robert Strickland, happily married to Rachel Kirby, smiled and waved as the couple danced by. Leland Myles, like Philip and Denton, was still available and tonight was actively pursuing Jessica Creighton.

Denton nudged Philip's ribs and said, "I see Leland is making cow eyes at your sister."

Philip watched as Leland smiled at Jessica, who lowered her eyes, as required by all proper young maidens. "He'll be sorry if he does catch her. Jessie can be a handful. She has an opinion, usually negative, about everything."

He recalled a conversation he had had with Jessica after one of Ursula's monthly socials earlier that year. At the time, he'd been amazed at how much she enjoyed the scandals and gossip about people's private lives. How, he had asked her, can such a sweet-looking young girl savor such muck-raking? She had gloated in reply that one learned the most amusing and useful tid-bits, and that she kept everything tucked away in her mind for later use.

"You are such a cynic," Denton teased, interrupting Philip's recollection. "Oh well, rather than watch everyone else having fun, I think I will ask one of these pretty girls to dance. Why don't you do the same?"

Philip made a face. "I would rather drown myself in the punch bowl. On the other hand," his gaze swept across the room to where Elizabeth waved her fan at an admirer, "I wouldn't mind taking that fetching bundle into my arms." Watching her intently through narrowed eyes, he said, as if to himself, "I've had this nagging feeling all evening that I have seen her before, but I can't remember where."

"One doesn't forget someone as lovely as that," Denton said, casting his own appreciative eye on their hostess.

"Oh well," Philip shrugged, "it will come to me in time."

"Are you perhaps a bit captivated by the lovely Miss Stockton?" Denton asked.

"Who am I," Philip chuckled, "that she should notice me in this room full of eligible young men? And that includes you, my friend." His eyes continued to follow her around the room. "How old did you say she is?"

"Eighteen, and just returned from a Philadelphia finishing school. I hear her father is very particular about who calls on her. Several gentlemen have indicated an interest in her but to her Papa's way of thinking," Denton winked, "they had no immediate prospects."

Philip gave his cravat a tug. "Perhaps Mr. Stockton prefers a more established gentleman, such as a publisher and banker."

Denton lowered his voice and said, "Don't look now, but I think she is coming this way."

Philip studied Elizabeth as she made her way across the room, smiling and acknowledging greetings from her guests. As she held her head in a particular way, with the candlelight reflected in her hazel eyes, an image from an October evening over a year ago--the night he first met Samantha--came into sharp focus. "Now I remember," he said, with a snap of his fingers. "She and her father were having dinner at the hotel. God, she was stunning."

Before Denton could respond, Elizabeth stood before them, flashing her most dazzling smile. "Mr. Philip Creighton, I believe."

"Your servant, Miss Stockton." Philip bowed over her hand. "Allow me to introduce my good friend, Denton Cobb."

Elizabeth acknowledged the introduction with a deep curtsy. "It is a pleasure to make your acquaintance, Mr. Cobb. And to be in the company of two such handsome gentlemen."

Denton shook the gloved hand she extended to him. "Good evening, Miss Stockton."

"Well, Mr. Creighton, it seems that we know one another without having been properly introduced. How very unconventional of me. And so naughty," she laughed. "Don't you agree, sir?"

"I have always found social convention a bit constraining."

She blushed behind her fan, but did not lower her gaze. "How gallant you are, sir, not to notice my bad manners."

He bowed again, looking deeply into those eyes that conveyed all sorts of invitations.

"Now that you are aware of how bold and ill-mannered I am, perhaps you will forgive me if I tell you both that I still have a few empty spaces on my dance card."

"Really? Well, we cannot have that. May I?" Philip took the card and penciled in his initials--PJC--with bold strokes. "There. I have filled in one space as well as claiming the pleasure of the last dance."

"Thank you, sir." She curtsied again, this time keeping her eyes lowered.

"Believe me, the pleasure is all mine," Philip murmured, but sensed no demure young miss here, even with the lowered eyes. Maybe she can make me forget. . . Stop it, he scolded himself, and simply admired her with unabashed fascination while Denton signed her dance card.

Sitting in a place of prominence at one end of the room to observe the comings and goings of the young people, Ursula Creighton watched the eagerly anticipated encounter between Philip and Elizabeth. She caught the eye of Elizabeth's father, Arthur Stockton, and saluted him with her cup of punch.

Arthur returned the gesture with his own cup.

Chapter 6

ELIZABETH SET A dizzying pace for herself and Philip during the Christmas social season. In mid-January, after a Sunday dinner at the Stockton home of rather poor fare and inferior wine, Arthur and Philip settled down by the fireplace to chat.

Grateful for this rare quiet moment, Philip took the opportunity to observe Arthur. He'd already decided that he would have a difficult time warming up to the man who could conceivably become his father-in-law. He found Arthur's demeanor insincere, and the man was too effusive with his compliments, too eager to please.

But Arthur's personal appearance belied any disconcerting feelings Philip may have had about him. Sitting here, all coziness and smiles, looking like someone's benevolent grandfather, he was shorter than Philip, rotund and completely bald, with a rosy complexion. His merry blue eyes made a person feel warm and smiled upon. His soft, pudgy hands offered proof that he had never done an honest day's work.

Arthur presents himself as a man of affairs. What exactly are those affairs? Philip asked himself. He makes veiled references to his out-of-town connections, to deals that are always pending, but he doesn't appear to have an establishment where he conducts those affairs.

Philip also noticed that wherever there was talk of money, Arthur was always present with his glad hand, ready cigar and a smile. Today, however, Arthur's eyes darted, his pudgy fingers twitched. Behind that carefully masked façade, Philip detected a sense of urgency. An urgency for what?

When the ladies joined them, Philip listened dutifully as Elizabeth played her latest accomplishment on the piano in a manner that would have caused the poor composer to pull his hair out in frustration.

Winter of 1860 had finally broken. March rains and dreary, muddy days gave way to a promising spring. By early April, crocuses peeked out from dormant flower gardens.

Ursula sat in her morning room, looking through the mail, oblivious to the beautiful spring morning. Clad in a soft lavender day frock, she was unmindful of the gardener just outside the window, preparing the flower beds for planting. At Philip's entrance, she glanced up with a smile.

"Good morning, Mother. May I speak with you a moment?"

"Of course, dear." She placed her pen in its crystal holder. "What is it?"

"Would you be agreeable to asking Elizabeth to join us for dinner this Sunday? I think it's time my family became better acquainted with her."

"A marvelous suggestion. I will send an invitation this afternoon. By the way," Ursula said, sounding unconcerned, "do you have any plans regarding yourself and this Stockton girl?"

Philip pursed his lips thoughtfully before nodding. "I have been giving it serious thought. What do you think of Elizabeth, Mother?"

Consider your answer carefully, Ursula reminded herself. A wrong word at this point could jeopardize everything. "She is lovely, if a bit flighty. However, I trust your judgment and will abide by whatever decision you make."

Philip gave her a questioning look before saying, "I may come to a decision before long. As for being flighty, Elizabeth is just high-spirited. Or perhaps a bit unsure of herself."

Ursula nearly strangled to keep from laughing out loud. Unsure? she thought. The only thing I have ever observed in the girl is cock-sure confidence. Aloud, she said, "That could be. Now, if you'll excuse me, I will write that note to Elizabeth. On second thought, I will include her parents in the invitation."

Across town, Arthur Stockton paced back and forth in the parlor, complaining to Elizabeth, "What is taking that Creighton whelp so long? My out-of-town creditors have been hounding me incessantly. They will not be put off much longer." He stopped in front of her. "I need access to Philip's money, and I need it now."

"Why not ask Philip for a loan if you are in such financial straits?" Elizabeth asked with a wave of dismissal.

Drawing himself up, Arthur regarded her with scorn. "I have my pride, missy. I am, after all, a gentleman. No, it has to be this way, with permanent access to all his wealth."

He continued pacing and waving his cigar. "And another thing, with so much at stake, we cannot afford to have Philip distracted by another female. I nearly had a heart attack when he began squiring that Ryder woman about. Fortunately for us, Ursula extricated him from that alliance before things got out of hand. Although, just how she accomplished it so swiftly, I cannot imagine." He stopped pacing and squinted at Elizabeth. "I know one thing for certain, I do not want that worthy matron as an adversary."

Elizabeth smiled at his panic. "Dear Papa, how you do go on. Rest assured that the deed will be accomplished before we have dinner with the Creightons this Sunday."

Two days later, Arthur Stockton puffed magnanimously on his cigar, while Elizabeth assessed herself critically in the mirror. Whirling around to face him, she flaunted the diamond ring under his nose. "Well, Papa, what do you think of your little girl now? I told you I would have Philip eating out of my hand before Sunday, and here is the proof."

"Well done, daughter." Admiring the size of the heart-shaped diamond, he calculated its cost. "Do you realize that we have pulled off the greatest coup in this blind little town's history? In fact, I believe Ursula herself did not know what we were about."

Elizabeth wriggled the fingers of her left hand so she could watch the diamond sparkle in the lamp light. "Have you made plans for all the money we will be getting?"

"Of course. There are some gentlemen I need to take care of first then we will set about spending the rest."

Elizabeth propped herself on the arm of Arthur's leather chair and asked with sudden concern, "Do you think Philip suspects?"

Arthur chuckled deep in his throat. "Put those thoughts from your mind, daughter. I know Philip's kind. I chose him for his damned sense of honor. While I, on the other hand, am not so burdened. I must, however, admit to one small twinge. It seems an awful lot to ask my little girl to give herself in marriage to a man she doesn't love." Clearing his throat, he continued with a stammer, "I hope you realize what marriage entails. I--I don't know how much your mother has told you, but your husband will have, uh, certain rights. If you are to maintain any control at all, you must be aware of those rights."

Elizabeth stood up and resumed preening before the mirror. "Of course, I'm aware of those rights, as you call them. I will take care of that when the time comes. If Philip bores me, I will look elsewhere for companionship."

Bolting from his chair, Arthur threw his half-smoked cigar into the fireplace. "Now see here, my girl, we will have none of that. I don't profess to be a prude, but you must remember yourself. It will not do." He shook a pudgy finger at her. "No, it simply will not do. You may amuse yourself but, for God's sake, be discreet. Who knows what Philip will resort to if he ever found out about such shenanigans."

She turned to face him, her demeanor calm. "Papa, please. Of course, I'll be discreet. Besides, who in this provincial little town would interest me?"

Arthur fell back into his chair, breathless. "I'm getting too old for this nonsense. Losing my nerve like that. Have you set the date?"

"Yes. Early August."

Arthur nodded approval. "I should be able to put off my creditors until then. Now, tell me, how did you accomplish this amazing feat in so short a time?"

"It was simple enough," she bragged. "I pouted and complained that we never spend any time alone. Of course, being anxious to please, he said we'd have a picnic and for me to wear my prettiest frock. After we drove out to a place by the river, he was all over me. Naturally, I clung to him, said what he wanted to hear, and dutifully batted my eyes."

Arthur watched the cigar smoke rise above his head. "How did you get him to agree to fork over the money for everything?"

"Oh, you would have been so proud of me," she cooed. "When he asked about setting the date, I appeared properly reticent about revealing matters of such a personal nature. I told him that you'd had some sort of reversal and were financially embarrassed. But being a lady and all, I didn't understand such things.

"This is where I really outdid myself," she said, laughing. "I told him that I felt a certain responsibility to wait until you could afford to give me a proper wedding. At that point, I looked up at him with tears in my eyes and said that I could not go to him without a dowry. The poor fool was putty in my hands."

Arthur laughed so hard, he almost swallowed his newly lit cigar. "What did he do then?"

"He fell all over himself saying that I must not worry, that he will lend you all the money you need and you can repay the loan when your finances are in order."

"Bravo, daughter," Arthur said, applauding her. "That is exactly how you maintain control."

Elizabeth wagged a finger at him. "Now remember, Papa, you must not say anything to Mother about the engagement. Philip wants to announce it at the Creighton's tomorrow."

"Of course, daughter." He returned her smile that sealed their conspiracy. "I cannot wait to see the expression on old lady Creighton's face when she hears about it.

Chapter 7

THE DAY OF the momentous dinner dawned cloudy, with a chilling wind that caused the temperatures to plummet. Philip, pacing and fidgety in the parlor, awaited the Stockton family's imminent arrival with Henry.

Philip stopped pacing long enough to say, "Pa, I can't say how happy I am that you are here today."

"Son," Henry said, relaxing in his favorite chair, a glass of bourbon in his right hand, "I would not have missed this dinner for anything."

The Stocktons arrived a few moments later, entering by the side door from the porte-cochere. Ursula greeted them with a broad smile. "Welcome, Arthur and Mary. My, my, the wind is quite nasty today, isn't it? Come into the parlor by the fire. We will have a spot of sherry to warm ourselves."

Philip waited until the maid had taken Elizabeth's shawl before taking her hand. He leaned close and whispered, "You didn't say anything, did you?"

Elizabeth shook her head. "I remembered our agreement and kept the ring hidden until I put on my gloves."

"Good." He squeezed her hand, pleased to have found someone so lovely after. . . None of that, he reminded himself.

George and Ellen arrived moments later, breathless and disheveled from the wind, as the maid was serving the sherry. Philip rose to introduce them. "Mr. and Mrs. Stockton, I'm sure you know my brother, George, and his wife, Ellen."

Mary Stockton smiled. "Yes, we have seen you in church. It is nice to see you again."

George and Ellen were expecting their second child later in the year but, as her condition was not yet obvious, Ursula permitted her presence at family functions. Ellen's morning sickness, as well as Ursula's stern admonitions, did not allow her to attend church services or other social functions.

Turning to Henry, Mary asked, "You have another son, don't you?"

"Yes," Henry nodded, "our youngest boy Matthew is away at the University of Virginia law school."

When the maid announced that dinner was served, the group moved to the dining room.

During the first course, Philip and Elizabeth could hardly keep their smiles from being noticed.

"All right, you two," Ursula said with a smile, "judging by all those meaningful glances, I can see that something is up. Share your little secret with the rest of us."

"Are we being that obvious?" Philip asked.

"Yes, you are," Jessica giggled. "Do tell."

Ellen and George exchanged confused glances with Mary Stockton.

"Shall we?" Elizabeth asked Philip with charming reticence.

"You tell them, dear."

"Somebody please tell us something," Henry chimed in with exasperated good humor.

"Yes," Arthur said, appearing befuddled. "What is going on?"

Standing, Philip took Elizabeth's hand and announced, "Elizabeth has honored me by accepting my proposal of marriage. We have set the wedding date for August."

With a smug smile, Elizabeth flashed her engagement ring around the table for all to see.

Henry shook Philip's hand and placed a perfunctory peck on Elizabeth's cheek. George congratulated him with a broad smile. Jessica swooped around the table to hug her future sister-in-law and admire the ring at close range. Ellen managed a wan smile, while barely concealing her envy of Elizabeth's ring.

Mary overcame her shyness long enough to express astonishment before giving her daughter a kiss. "This is quite a surprise, dear. I had no idea. I'm sure you and Philip will be very happy."

Arthur clapped Philip on the back. "You are a sly one, my boy. Surprising us like this. You have my blessing." Turning to the others, still talking and offering best wishes to Elizabeth, he said, "Allow me to propose a toast to the happy couple. A long and prosperous life to you both." Raising his wineglass, he shot Ursula a triumphant glance.

"Philip," Ursula cooed, "how clever of you to court this sweet girl-- and right under our very noses. Elizabeth, darling, come here."

Ursula reached out her arms to welcome her future daughter-in-law.

Chapter 8

SITTING NEXT TO Philip on the train, her cold hand clasped firmly in his, Elizabeth fought the urge to snatch her hand away and scream at him to leave her alone. Not yet, she reminded herself. Some day. But not now.

Instead, she gave Philip the benefit of her most devastating smile and squeezed his hand.

"Your hands are cold, sweetheart. Are you nervous about meeting my uncle and his family?" he asked.

"A bit. Do your two families get together like this every year?"

"We have celebrated Independence Day with Uncle Ben and Aunt Helen for as long as I can remember," Matthew, the youngest Creighton son, said with a smile. Enjoying his summer vacation away from college, he sat in the seat facing them. "We usually eat too much, play too hard, and drink too much beer. Also, Uncle Ben raises the best Arabians in Maryland, so people from New England, Virginia, Kentucky, and even European nobility come to buy his horses. He has a reputation for the fastest racers and best breeders."

"How exciting," she responded with a stifled yawn. "Do they have any children?"

"Yes," Philip nodded, "a son and a daughter. Maggie, the youngest, is fifteen years old, a year younger than Jessica. Not only is she pretty, she has a sweet disposition. But the poor child is rather frail, a result of scarlet fever."

"And her brother?" she asked, hoping he wasn't as boring as these Creightons.

She noticed the slightest variation in Philip's voice when he said, "Julian is my age. Everyone says we resemble one another but personally, I can't see it. All the ladies think he is handsome, so naturally, he is the darling of the family. In fact," he lowered his voice, "it has been rumored within the family that he's had to fend off several irate husbands. Or so I have been told," he added in response to her shocked reaction. "Of course, that sort of thing is only whispered about."

Glancing beyond Elizabeth's shoulder, he pointed out the train window, "There's Uncle Ben now. The one with the gray hair and big grin."

She turned to observe the man waving to them from the platform. "He doesn't look at all like your father, does he?"

"No two brothers could be more dissimilar in looks, tastes or temperament," Matthew said. "Pa is the quiet one. You never know what he's thinking. In a moment, you'll see that Uncle Ben is his direct opposite."

"Yes," Philip agreed. "He is outgoing, boisterous, and has large hands that are no strangers to hard work. I've always thought that he must be the happiest man I have ever met." Running his hand over his hair, he added with a smile, "He and I have the same unruly hair that tends to turn white at a rather early age."

Outside on the platform, Benjamin Creighton greeted his brother Henry with a handshake, and placed a kiss in the air near Ursula's cheek. He and Matthew shook hands then he engulfed Jessica in one of his hardy embraces. Philip felt the bones in his hand give way under his uncle's grip before saying, "Uncle, I would like to present my fiancée, Miss Elizabeth Stockton. My dear, this is my Uncle Benjamin."

Elizabeth bobbed the requisite curtsy and murmured, "Mr. Creighton. I'm so happy to meet you at last. Philip has told me how much he admires you."

"My dear Miss Stockton," Benjamin boomed. "Welcome to our home and to the family."

Caught unawares, Elizabeth resigned herself to having the breath squeezed from her lungs.

"Well, nephew," Ben said, turning to Philip, "you have out-done yourself with this beauty. Come, come, everyone," he continued, gesturing to the cabbies, "I have hired two hacks to accommodate you and your luggage."

Once everyone was situated in Benjamin's carriage and the hacks, the entourage made its way through the rolling Maryland countryside. Elizabeth found the trip hot and dusty, and Philip's constant chatter about his family frayed her nerves nearly to the breaking point. Gritting her teeth, she pretended to listen to every word.

About half an hour later, they turned into the long driveway leading to the house. "Here we are at last," Philip said. "You will love Aunt Helen. She has a knack for making everyone feel at ease."

I'm sure, Elizabeth thought, *although she sounds too domestic for my tastes.*

Helen and Maggie were standing on the front porch of the rambling, two-story farmhouse, watching as the cabs pulled into the circular driveway. After exchanging greetings, Helen inquired of Ursula, "Will George and Ellen be arriving soon?"

"They were unable to accompany us this year," Ursula sniffed. "Ellen's condition does not permit her to travel abroad."

Blushing with mortification, Helen clucked, "Oh, dear, I'm so sorry. Perhaps next year."

"Perhaps," Ursula replied through compressed lips.

"Hello, dear," Helen said after being introduced to Elizabeth, and hugged her with genuine warmth. "We are so happy you could join us. This is our daughter, Maggie."

Smiling shyly, Maggie curtsied before extending her hand. "Welcome, Elizabeth."

"Come into the house, dear," Helen said, slipping an arm around Elizabeth's waist. "You will want to freshen up after that nasty train ride. Come, Ursula and Jessica," she called over her shoulder, "we will have a nice visit after you have changed. It is such a lovely day that I decided we would have supper out here under the trees."

With one arm around Elizabeth and the other around Jessica, she led the ladies to their respective rooms. Jessica went directly to Maggie's room while Matthew was assigned to Julian's room. Philip was given the downstairs back bedroom.

Maggie led Elizabeth to a dormer room directly across the hall from Henry and Ursula. Not a very subtle hint, Elizabeth thought with a grim smile. But they needn't worry. I have no urgent desire to go downstairs and ravage their darling son.

Taking off her grimy frock, she splashed her face and arms with cool water in the wash basin, then lay on the bed for a few moments. How nice it is, she thought with a grateful sigh, to lie on something that doesn't jolt or spew cinders.

Once she'd recovered herself, she got up and powdered her arms and breasts and put on a clean yellow dress trimmed with white lace that set off her hazel eyes to perfection. Picking up her straw hat, she started down the stairs.

When she saw a female slave bustling about the kitchen, Elizabeth realized she'd taken the back stairs instead of the main staircase. Without acknowledging the woman's existence, she turned to leave but was startled to see a young man leaning against the doorjamb. His looks were strikingly similar to Philip's. He was slender, with dark hair and eyes, and a grin that betrayed his thoughts--thoughts that made Elizabeth want to blush. In that regard, she thought, he's not at all like Philip.

"You must be Julian," she managed to stammer.

"Your most humble servant." Bowing, he smiled at her in the most disarming way. "And you, I presume, are my future cousin Elizabeth. May I offer you a cool drink? Mandy makes the most delicious lemonade in all of Maryland. We even have ice," he added, jiggling his glass. He told the kitchen slave, Mandy, to pour some lemonade, then personally dropped several pieces of ice into the glass.

"Now," he said, handing the lemonade to Elizabeth, "shall we go onto the side porch, away from that gaggle of tongues out front? We can get better acquainted that way." Following her out the door, he commented in his sultry voice, "My, you are an exquisite creature, Miss Elizabeth. Much too good for Philip, I'll warrant."

"You are too kind, sir," she said, giving him the benefit of her own smile. "But you must not say such naughty things about Philip."

Julian waved off her admonition. "Let's not talk about boring old Philip. I would much rather talk about you. You are much more fascinating, and you smell so good."

Elizabeth smiled her thanks as she preceded him onto the side porch. The U-shaped porch ran from the side door at the kitchen to the front of the house and around to the back bedroom on the other side. Lounging against the railing, Julian smiled at her over the rim of his glass.

Meeting his dark look with a seductive one of her own, she asked, "Do you help your father with the farm and the horses?"

Julian threw back his head and laughed. "Me? Work on a farm? No, I am the bane of my father's existence. I would like to make my way somewhere else, preferably in Washington. But," he added with a shrug, "as luck would have it, I have no money of my own and, alas, no talents. So, here I will stay until Lady Luck arranges something agreeable for me."

Elizabeth bit her lip to keep from laughing. She was casting about in her mind for something noncommittal to say when Philip appeared at the front corner of the porch. Even at this distance, she could see his jaw muscles flexing, a sure sign that he was disturbed.

Philip walked briskly toward her. "I see you two have met," he commented coolly to Julian, after placing a possessive kiss on Elizabeth's forehead. "Well, what do you think of my lady? Isn't she lovely?"

Julian suppressed a smirk before responding, "You have outdone yourself, cousin. I have even warranted to Elizabeth that she is undoubtedly much too good for you."

Stamping her foot, Elizabeth stuck out a petulant lip. "I will not be talked about as though I were a statue."

"I'm sorry, my dear." Putting his arms around her, Philip looked into her darkened eyes. "I meant no offense."

"My dear Elizabeth," Julian said with a mocking bow, "I am desolate for having offended you. My deepest apologies."

Unable to resist the wicked smile she saw twitching at the corners of Julian's lips, she relented. "Oh, all right."

With her arm linked through Philip's, and still carrying her glass of lemonade, they joined the others at the front of the house.

At Elizabeth's approach, the gentlemen jumped up to offer her a seat. "Thank you, gentlemen, but if Maggie doesn't mind, I will sit next to her on the chaise lounge so we can chat and get better acquainted."

"May I see your engagement ring?" Maggie asked, her eyes fairly bulging at the heart-shaped diamond.

"I hadn't noticed a ring, Elizabeth. May I?" Julian asked.

"Of course." She gladly obliged by extending her left hand toward him.

"My, what an enormous bauble." Leaning closer to examine the ring, he whispered, "I trust you have already planned how you will spend the rest of Philip's money."

Unnerved by how adept Julian was at unmasking her intentions toward Philip, Elizabeth snatched her hand away from his grasp. "Thank you, Julian."

Composing herself, she turned with a forced smile to engage Maggie in conversation.

Chapter 9

THE NEXT DAY, Independence Day, dawned sunny and hot, perfect weather for the annual race between one of Ben's Arabians and his neighbor John Mitchell's prized horse ridden by his son, Peter. Matthew volunteered to ride for his Uncle Ben again this year.

Once the course was set, Philip fired the gun to start the race. The two horses raced neck in neck down to the main gate, turned, and sped back toward the silo in back of the house, with the Mitchell horse pulling ahead of Ben's horse by a nose. They galloped stride for stride around the silo, past the barn and back to the front of the house, a distance of over a mile.

Philip stood beside Elizabeth, his arm firmly around her waist. During the race, he became excited and urged Matthew on. Uninterested, Elizabeth kept her eyes on Julian who stood under a weeping willow tree, sipping beer. She flushed when he saluted her with his glass.

Matthew roared across the finish line inches ahead of Peter Mitchell. Delirious with joy, Ben poured beer for his male guests. Talk among the men continued on horses, the weather and crops. Gradually, inevitably, the conversation turned to the heated issues of the day--abolition and

States Rights. Tempers flared. No one could remain calm or objective while discussing these subjects, especially in a state as predominantly Southern in its sympathies as Maryland is.

Fanning herself lazily, Elizabeth strolled away from the raucous group. Men are so boring, she sighed to herself. Always getting themselves all worked up over slavery and war and such nonsense. Perhaps Julian will relieve my boredom.

She found him still under the willow tree, drawing a beer for a dejected Peter Mitchell. She observed Maggie standing close to Peter, gazing up at him with a shy smile. My, my, she thought, do we have a budding romance here?

"Would you care for something cold to drink, cousin Elizabeth?" Smiling his most wicked smile, Julian offered her a beer.

"Some lemonade, thank you," she replied with pursed lips.

They sat in the lawn chairs partially hidden by the drooping willow branches that swayed gently in the hot breeze. "Do you love him?" Julian asked with a wicked grin.

Elizabeth turned innocent eyes on him. "Why, Julian, what a question."

"Well, do you?" he pressed, and inched his chair closer to hers.

"I am going to marry him."

"Marrying someone does not necessarily mean you are in love with that person."

"You, sir, are impertinent," she sniffed in haughty disapproval.

"Stop evading the issue, Miss, and answer my question."

She took a sip of lemonade before replying, "It should be obvious how I feel about Philip."

"It is perfectly obvious to me, if to no one else, how you feel about the poor fool. That is why I cannot help wondering why you are marrying Philip. Is it his money?"

"Really, Julian, I consider this conversation rather vulgar."

He leaned closer. "If I had as much money as Philip, would you marry me?"

"Is that a proposal?" she asked, as bright yellow flecks danced in her hazel eyes.

"No. Merely conjecture on my part." He kept his eyes fixed on her. "Well, would you?"

"Probably not," she said with a jerk of her chin. "It might ruin our lovely friendship."

Leaning back in his chair, Julian laughed out loud. "By God, Elizabeth, what I like best about you is your candor. "You are right, of course. We should not ruin our friendship with anything as mundane as marriage. I believe we can enjoy one another without benefit of clergy."

"Julian!" She tapped his arm with her fan. "You don't believe I'd really do such a thing."

"It is a lovely thought, isn't it?" Suddenly, the smile left his eyes. "Uh, oh, our fun is over. The groom-to-be approaches."

Philip strode into their midst, went straight to Elizabeth's chair and clasped her free hand in his. "This conversation sounds far more entertaining than the one I was engaged in. I see you find my fiancée amusing, Julian."

"Yes, very." Julian rose and bowed ever so slightly. "If you will excuse me, I will leave you two love birds alone." He sauntered off, grinning to himself.

Philip sat in the chair vacated by Julian. "Are you having a good time, dear?"

"Oh, yes," she assured him. Rising, she offered Philip her hand. "Shall we join the others?"

"Your hands are cold, sweetheart. Is something wrong? Nervous, perhaps?"

Suppressing a frown, she demurred, "No. It must be the ice in my lemonade."

"I will warm them for you."

"Please, Philip," she protested in a sharp voice, "let go of me. I think we should join the others now." She walked away, leaving Philip with little choice but to follow.

At sunset, the slaves cleared the tables to make room for the ice cream makers while the men began setting up the fireworks to shoot off after dark.

Henry took a seat beside Philip on the porch swing and accepted a light for his cigar. "Thank you, son. You seem happy."

"Yes, Pa, I could not be happier."

"I hope you know what you are doing, marrying that Stockton girl. Something about her does not strike me quite right."

Philip turned toward his father. "What makes you say that?"

"Nothing specific. It's just--oh hell, maybe I am beyond all this romantic nonsense." He patted Philip's knee and rose to leave. "I just want you to be happy, son."

"Thanks, Pa," Philip replied, still puzzled. Watching Henry walk away, he wondered what made his usually reticent father ask such personal questions.

Shaking his head, he turned back to the croquet game between Jessica, Elizabeth, Maggie and Peter Mitchell that had apparently broken up during his conversation with his father. He glanced around the busy yard, searching for Elizabeth. Oh well, he decided with a shrug, she must have gone into the house.

"Philip," Helen called from the yard, "would you please go into the house and tell Mandy to bring out more rock salt?"

"Certainly, Aunt Helen." Snuffing out his cheroot, he headed inside to the kitchen. After giving Mandy the message, he started back down the hall. Outside the back bedroom door, he heard a giggle. Grinning, he surmised that Peter must have brought Maggie inside to steal a kiss.

Philip continued toward the front door when he heard Elizabeth's voice. "Stop, you are taking my breath away." Another giggle, followed by the low moaning sound of pleasure.

"Shhh. Mandy will hear you." Julian's voice. "Turn this way so I can reach that button."

Overwhelmed by the sickening realization that Julian had seduced Elizabeth, Philip slumped against the wall, unmindful of perspiration breaking out under his shirt. Time and time again, he recalled with disgust, *she shunned my kisses but is more than willing to let that damned rascal do whatever he wants with her.* The familiar feeling of being rejected, first by Samantha, and now possibly by Elizabeth, engulfed him. *No! Not again--and not to Julian.*

He burst into the bedroom, yanked Julian from Elizabeth's arms and slammed him against the wall. Pressing his forearm against Julian's throat, he growled, "By God, I'll kill you for this."

"Get hold of yourself, old man," Julian said in a strangled voice. Recovering himself, he smirked as he shoved Philip away. "It was just a little romp. It meant nothing."

Philip shoved Julian back, thumping his head against the wall. "Damn it, is everything just a trifle with you?"

They scuffled, with neither gaining the advantage. Elizabeth sat in the middle of the bed, clutching her gaping bodice together and watching in horror. Philip broke free of Julian's grip and swung at him, landing a glancing blow off his shoulder. Julian fell back but Philip grabbed him again. As he brought his fist around to smash it into Julian's face, someone gripped his wrist and stepped between them.

"No, don't do this, Massah Philip," Mandy pleaded. "You don't wanna make Miz Helen and Massah Benjamin shamed in front of their company. He ain't worth it," she said, jerking her chin in Julian's direction.

"Damn you, Mandy," Julian said through clenched teeth, "I will sell you South for that."

"Shut up, you bastard," Philip shouted back. Running a hand over his sweaty face, he said in a hoarse voice, "Thanks, Mandy. The last thing I want is to embarrass my aunt and uncle." Turning back to his cousin, he brought his face close to Julian's, his eyes so fierce that Julian could not help but flinch. "I will repay you for this. Maybe not tonight. Or even tomorrow. But rest assured, it will happen."

Helen's voice down the hall shattered the tense moment. "Mandy, did you find the salt?"

Mandy stuck her head out the bedroom door and called, "Yes'um, Miz Helen, I got it right here." Glancing around frantically, she asked, "Now, where'd I drop that rock salt?"

Philip leaned his sweaty forehead against the doorjamb while Mandy looked for the salt, then heard her retreating voice say, "Comin', Miz Helen."

Julian slumped into a chair, coughing and gagging to recover from Philip's choke-hold.

Philip stalked over to the bed where Elizabeth hurriedly smoothed her skirts. He fixed a gaze on her that was at once wounded and unforgiving. "As for you, Miss Stockton, I will not hold you to your pledge to marry me." He walked out before she could react.

Hearing him slam out the side door, Elizabeth broke into hysterical sobs. "Oh, my God, look at what you have done," she cried to Julian. "Everything is in ruins."

Julian ran over to the bed and shook her until her curls came loose and fell about her face. "Get hold of yourself, you fool. Don't lose your composure now."

She looked up at him, tears blurring her vision. "What do you mean?"

"Go out there and say, or do, whatever is necessary to get him back. You don't want to miss out on becoming Mrs. Philip Creighton and all that goes with it, do you?" Julian asked in a significant tone, his meaning quite clear.

Slowly, her panic subsided and comprehension set in. "Give me a moment to collect my thoughts." After running several options through her mind, she said, "I will tell him it was all your doing. That you seduced me. I didn't know what was happening."

"Tell him whatever you please. It is already his firmly held belief that I am a bastard. Of course, I don't think much of him either. He is such a proper gentleman."

She turned hard eyes on him. "Please remember, my dear Julian, we are relying on his being a 'proper gentleman' to accept and believe whatever I choose to tell him. But first, I will need to do something about my appearance. Is there a hair brush on the dresser?"

Stepping onto the side porch a few moments later, Elizabeth scanned the dark yard. She spied Philip in the orchard, leaning against a cherry tree and staring at the high-spirited crowd in the front yard. Steeling herself, she picked her way across the dew-laden grass as fireflies blinked in the darkness. A sharp report from the fireworks surprised her and she cried out.

Startled, Philip called, "Who's there?"

"Philip, dear," she answered in a trembling voice, "it is I."

He turned away from her. "I prefer to be alone just now."

"Listen to me, Philip," she pleaded into his rigid back. Against the fireworks illuminating the front yard, she could see his jaw muscles flexing. Her resolved wavered. "I came to beg your forgiveness," she said in a conciliatory voice. "It was all Julian's fault. He seduced me and, like a fool, I followed him before I realized what he had in mind."

Touching his arm tentatively, she added, "Then when I saw how angry and hurt you were, I was so mortified, I wanted to die."

He recoiled from her touch. "Of course I was hurt and angry. You allowed Julian to take liberties but you put me off if I so much as touch your hand."

"I behaved that way because I knew that having a lady for a wife was important to you. I did not want you to think ill of me." She quivered her chin. "I cannot imagine what you must think of me now."

After a long and terrible pause, he answered, "I am no longer sure of that myself."

Shaken by the harshness in his voice, her resolve strengthened. "You must believe that I have never wanted to marry anyone but you. Not Julian. Just you," she added in a whisper.

"I believed that before--before tonight."

Sensing the hesitation in his voice, she thought, Good, he's weakening. I must strike now, while he is still wrestling with his emotions. "I admit that tonight could have been a horrible mistake," she said, looking properly contrite. "The only thing I could think while you were fighting with Julian was that I might lose you--all because of a few thoughtless moments."

She pressed her check against his back. "Oh, Philip, I can't lose you. You mean too much to me. I know I have no right to ask, but I beg you, please give me another chance." She walked around to face him and slid her arms around his neck. "I have never wanted anyone but you. No one," she added, and pressed her lips against his.

Philip pulled away from her embrace and sat on the ground. "I don't want to make any decisions just now. I am still angry but more than that, I am shocked by my own reaction to the situation. I cannot explain it but it was as if someone else had taken control of me," he said in wonder. "I actually wanted to kill Julian."

Still determined to prevail, she sat beside him on the damp grass. "This whole ordeal has been a nightmare for both of us, darling. Thank God, you prevented me from making a mistake that could have ruined both our lives."

Acting as though she had said nothing, he stared up at the fireworks exploding overhead and leaving an acrid smell in the humid night air. "We will not speak of it any more tonight," he said at last. "I need to be alone--to think. However, you were right about one thing. I do expect my wife to be a lady. But, after what I witnessed tonight, I have some serious issues to sort though."

Undaunted by his rejection, she plunged ahead. "I admit that what I did tonight was lacking in good judgment. But I promise you, I will spend the rest of my life making it up to you."

Standing abruptly, he thrust his fists into his pockets. "That may not be an option much longer."

She clutched at his arm in desperation. "But I don't want to be released from our betrothal."

"I told you, I need time to put everything into perspective."

As the crowd ooh-ed and aah-ed at the last grand burst of fireworks, fear gripped her heart. 'Say or do whatever is necessary to get him back,' Julian had urged. 'Control, daughter, control,' Papa had repeated. She lifted her eyes, eyes that were hard and determined, and said in her best wheedling voice, "Philip, sweetheart, it frightens me when you talk like that."

"I will inform you of my decision," he said tersely, and stalked toward the house.

She watched him go, his back erect, fists clenched at his sides. Dropping to her knees, she pounded the ground with her fists and wailed, "Damn you, Julian. You said Philip would never do anything but you underestimated him. So did I. Now what am I going to do?

"Oh, Papa is going to kill me."

Chapter 10

FINALLY, MERCIFULLY, THE picnic was over.

After the last guest had departed, Philip retreated to the shadows at the far end of the porch and waited to see what happened next between Elizabeth and Julian. After pretending to help his father and a male slave for a few moments, Julian stretched into a theatrical yawn.

"If everyone will excuse me," Julian said, "I'm going to bed. It's been a long day."

Yes, Philip thought with a wry smile, you must be tired after all the havoc you've wreaked today. He watched Elizabeth stroll into the house with Maggie and Jessica, laughing and chatting about Maggie's romantic escapade with Peter Mitchell. Disheartened, he wondered how she could carry on as though nothing had happened.

Ursula interrupted his turbulent thoughts. "Are you coming to bed, Philip?"

"I will be along in a moment, Mother."

"After all the heat and noise today," she complained, "my head is about explode. What about you, Helen?"

"Yes," Helen nodded, looking drained by the day's activities. "I believe I will call it a day too. Good night all."

"Good night, Mother. Aunt Helen," Matthew said, as he mounted the porch steps to join them. To Philip he said, "Do you want another beer?"

"No, thanks. I'm going to finish my cheroot and turn in."

"All right. I will just drink this beer then visit the necessary. I've had quite a few already," Matthew added with a sheepish grin. "But I think I earned it after my victory today."

"Yes, you did," Philip agreed, and forced a smile. He watched Matthew detour on his way to the necessary to exchange a few words with their father and Uncle Ben.

A moment later, Henry climbed the steps and peered across the dark porch. "Philip, is that you?" he asked in an unsure voice.

"Yes, sir."

"Are you all right, son?"

After a long silence, Philip answered in a strangled voice, "Yes, Pa, I'm fine."

"I see." Henry paused for a moment, as though considering something, then nodded. "I will see you in the morning."

"Good night Pa. Good night, Uncle Ben. Congratulations on winning the race again."

"Thank you, Philip," Benjamin beamed.

After everyone had gone into the house, Philip remained on the porch, pondering his dilemma. *Am I making a mistake by marrying Elizabeth after what transpired this evening? All day, her eyes seemed to follow Julian everywhere. No matter where I looked, they were always together. Damn it. Things have always gone Julian's way. From the time we were young boys, he always made a point of pulling some prank then placing the blame on me.*

But this wasn't a boyish prank. He seduced Elizabeth so he could flaunt it in my face. He must always prevail, no matter who gets hurt. The feelings of others mean nothing to him.

Oh God, Philip groaned to himself, *I can't let him prevail. Not this time.*

The familiar pain of Samantha's rejection flooded over him. *I can't go through that again. I may never know what caused Samantha to* leave me but I can learn from my mistake and do something about this hellish situation.

Philip stared into the quiet night, pondering his options.

At Crossroads two days later, Philip stood before the cheval mirror in his bedroom, assessing his haggard appearance that was accentuated by dark circles under his eyes from lack of sleep. Elizabeth's desperate words of devotion in the orchard that night still rang in his ears. Were they true? Or were her declarations hollow?

But it was the image of Julian pawing Elizabeth, and his cavalier attitude about the entire episode that thwarted all attempts at sleep. *That bastard seduced her so he could show me how easy it was to take any woman at any time. Damn him. I should have known better than to take Elizabeth with us to Uncle Ben's.*

But, by God, he-- A knock at the door broke into his thoughts.

A moment later, Matthew poked his head into Philip's bedroom. "May I come in? I need to speak with you."

Philip stopped fighting with the knot in his cravat. "Certainly, Matt."

"If you are on your way out, I can come back later."

"I was planning to call on Elizabeth, but that can wait." Philip frowned, sensing by his brother's downcast appearance that something was not right.

Very much like Philip in height and looks, Matthew's hair was not as dark as the other Creighton men, and his black eyes revealed a gentle nature. While both brothers smiled easily, Matthew's smile revealed the sensitive, thoughtful man within.

"You look as if you have something serious on your mind. What is it?" Philip asked, giving Matthew's shoulder a nudge with his fist. "Girl troubles?"

"You could say that," Matthew replied, not responding to Philip's attempt at lightening his mood. "Do you remember my telling you that I have been seeing the sister of my college classmate? You know, Luke Hilling's sister, Polly."

"Judging by the expression on your face, I suspect that something is amiss between you and Polly Hilling."

"You could say that. Her father. He is a staunch supporter of States' Rights, which has led to some rather heated discussions during my visits."

"How did you handle it?"

"Usually by side-stepping the issues with evasive answers, or by keeping silent. But I can't continue that much longer. As much as I care for Polly, I am not sure we can build a future with this divisive issue between us. I must be true to my own convictions, which are diametrically opposed to Mr. Hilling's. Naturally, he does not want his daughter involved with a Northerner, especially an out-spoken advocate of rights for all."

Matthew dropped into a chair. "I'm torn between my affection for Polly on the one hand and my principles on the other. If we were to marry, I don't know how she would feel about living in Pennsylvania. I doubt that Mr. Hilling would allow her to leave Virginia, and I certainly cannot live there. Not after all the cruelty I've witnessed firsthand.

"I have seen my classmates mistreat their personal slaves whom they believe have no minds or feelings. Families are separated with no consideration for fathers, mothers or their babies. They are worked beyond human endurance and beaten for the slightest infraction, real or imagined."

"What does your heart tell you, Matt?"

"My heart wants Polly, and I have every reason to believe that she cares for me too."

"How does Polly feel about the issues you mentioned?"

"She thinks slavery is all right because it has been that way for as long as she can remember. She says her grandparents have always had slaves. 'What's wrong with it?' she asks me when I bring it up. 'What would the darkies be doing if they weren't working for Father?' I tried telling her that families should be kept together instead of being torn apart and sold like cattle. And that the whole institution of slavery is immoral. Against everything that is right and decent."

Philip pondered a moment before saying, "I am sure you realize that these issues cannot be avoided if you expect to have a future with Polly. They must be settled--soon. "

"I know, I know," Matthew groaned. He stood and began pacing back and forth at the foot of Philip's four-poster bed, his hands clasped behind him. "If I didn't care so much for her, I would turn my back on it all. But, damn it, I do care. I care about the slavery issue. And I care very deeply for Polly. As you can see, these two areas appear irreconcilable."

"Do you have a plan in mind?"

"I plan to go to Virginia in August, before the school term begins, to see if Polly and I can find some middle ground where we can love one another without allowing these issues to come between us." He turned to Philip, his expression hopeful. "What do you think?"

"It appears you have no other choice. If that strategy proves unsuccessful, at least you have made every effort to win her without disregarding her sensitivities."

Matthew gave him a grateful smile. "Thanks for the confirmation, Philip. I will write to Polly right away and tell her to expect me in mid-August." He paused at the door before leaving. "I knew I could count on you. You always seem to have your own life in such good order."

Grimacing at the irony in Matthew's remark, Philip waved him off.

After Matthew closed the door, Philip shook his head, thinking, poor Matt may be embarking on a fool's errand but there isn't a damned thing I, or anyone else, can do about it.

Some things a man must discover for himself.

Giving his cravat a final tug, he muttered aloud, "I should know. I am about to set out on my own fool's errand."

Arriving at the Stockton home a few minutes after eight o'clock, Philip was shown into the parlor. He instructed the maid that he and Elizabeth were not to be disturbed for any reason. She curtsied and went off to fetch the young mistress.

Elizabeth entered a few moments later, looking pale, her eyes red and puffy. "Hello, Philip," she said in a formal tone, and indicated that he take a chair. "Would you like some refreshment?"

"Nothing, thank you." After they were both seated, Philip cleared his throat and began in a firm voice, "Elizabeth, I will get right to the point. I have done a great deal of soul searching these past two days and have come to a decision." He held up his hand to discourage her response. "Let me speak my piece before you say anything."

She folded her trembling hands in her lap and waited for him to continue.

"I realize that you are young and inexperienced, and cannot be blamed entirely for that unpleasant episode at Uncle Ben's. Julian, on the other hand, is well practiced in the ways of seducing women."

As he spoke, he noticed that Elizabeth had fallen against the back of her chair instead of maintaining a rigid posture as etiquette demanded. Her eyes had widened with his every word.

Despite the knot in his stomach, he continued, "Forgive me for being so blunt, but I must be honest with you. I feel it is only proper that I not hold you to your promise. There is still time to cancel the wedding plans. The decision is entirely up to you."

"I swear to you, Philip," Elizabeth cried, "nothing happened. I let Julian kiss me but then I became frightened. I didn't know how to stop him. He is not the gentleman you are. Oh, how could I have been so foolish?" she moaned. "It was a childish, impetuous thing to do."

In one swift motion, she slid from her chair and knelt at his feet, her skirts forming a circle around her. She clutched his hands in hers. "Believe me, darling, you are the man I want to marry. No one else."

Seeing tears in those pleading eyes, Philip felt his resolve crumble, and wondered how he could have doubted her sincerity. He pulled her onto his lap and kissed her tenderly. "Marriage is a serious matter. Are you certain about this?"

"Oh, yes," she answered, and tightened her embrace. "More certain than I have ever been of anything in my life." She snuggled against his chest and squeezed more tears from her eyes. Pressing her lips against the warm spot on his throat, she whispered, "I have been so fearful of losing you that I have cried constantly these last two days."

He responded by kissing her ardently this time. To his delight, she returned his kisses more eagerly than ever before.

After a moment, she drew away from him. "Please, darling, let me catch my breath. What would Papa say if he caught us like this?"

"Maybe he will get his shotgun and force me to marry you right away."

Chapter 11

ON THE MORNING of her wedding, Elizabeth pulled aside the shabby lace curtains on her bedroom window and gazed with amusement at the frantic scene on the lawn below. Hotel caterers scurried about, arranging the tables and chairs, and setting up the dance platform.

Mary Stockton hurried into her daughter's room at that moment, breathless and fussing. "Goodness, Elizabeth, haven't you finished your *toilet* yet?"

"Stop fretting, Mother. There is plenty of time."

Mary glanced through the window at the sky. "Those dark clouds look rather menacing. Oh, why did I let you and your father convince me that holding this wedding out of doors was a good idea?"

"Oh, pooh, Mother. You worry too much. All will be well today, no matter what the weather. Once Philip slips that ring on my finger, I will achieve the highest social status of any woman in Crossroads," Elizabeth paused, her eyes darkening, "with the exception of my dear mother-in-law, of course."

"You will remember yourself today, won't you, dear?" Mary pleaded, and dabbed at the moisture on her upper lip. "Promise me that you will not do anything untoward."

"Believe me, Mother, I will do nothing to mar the glory of this day. Now," she added, nudging Mary out the door, "why don't you go down and help Papa. He has already made the caterers adjust the floral arrangements several times."

At the Creighton home, the Henry and Benjamin Creighton families, along with a few close friends, gathered for a champagne brunch. Ellen, pale and ill with morning sickness, was permitted to attend the breakfast, after carefully concealing her pregnancy. Ursula had declared the week before that, given Ellen's advanced condition, attending the wedding was out of the question.

Philip seated himself on the same side of the table as Julian, but at the opposite end where his father, Matthew, Uncle Ben and Congressman Catlett sat. I am in no mood today for Julian's smirks and barbs, he thought. Let George and Ellen deal with him. And Mother.

"My dear Miss Millicent," he said to Congressman Catlett's pudgy sister sitting across the table from him, "what is the latest gossip in Washington City?"

He and Miss Millicent had carried on an unspoken, and quite innocent, flirtation these last few years. He found her outspoken manner delightful and refreshing. She was also safe, being a maiden lady of unquestioned standing and reputation. And he enjoyed her company.

"Well," she began, eyeing a platter of ham the maid held before her, "the whole town is abuzz about this secession nonsense. I cannot imagine what those southerners are thinking."

"Perhaps cooler heads will prevail, and we can avoid what some feel is inevitable."

"I pray you are right, dear boy. But," she waved her fork in dismissal, "I try not to bother my head about such things. I leave that to the gentlemen. Will you pass the biscuits, dear?" Miss Millicent buttered a biscuit and accepted more coffee from the maid. After taking a sip, she made a satisfied face and continued, "Do you suppose all this talk of secession will stir up some sort of unpleasantness?"

Before Philip could reply, Ursula interrupted smoothly, "How wise you are, Miss Millicent, to leave these matters to the gentlemen. Would you like more coffee cake?"

Catching Ursula's meaningful look, Henry engaged Ben and Congressman Catlett in a discussion of a less volatile nature.

Philip turned to Matthew on his right. "You have been rather quiet since you got home from school Friday night."

"Have I?" Matthew asked, pushing his Eggs Benedict around on the plate.

"I meant to inquire about your visit with Miss Hilling but I've been deluged with so many wedding details."

Matthew twirled the stem of his champagne glass between his fingers but remained silent.

Concerned, Philip sat his coffee cup in its saucer. "What happened, Matt?"

He leaned closer to Philip and said barely above a whisper, "As I feared, Mr. Hilling forced me into a position of defending my principles. Then he became furious and informed me that I am never to contact Polly again."

"What will you do now?"

"What can I do?" Matthew shrugged. "Her brother Luke is sympathetic, but he doesn't dare go against his father's wishes. When Polly writes to Luke at school, she smuggles in a note for me. Besides a few coded messages from me in his letters to her, it is the only contact we have."

"Have you considered asking her to marry you?"

"Yes, but she would be ostracized from her family. I am not willing to ask Polly to pay such a price."

"I'm so sorry," Philip whispered. "Perhaps I shouldn't have advised you to force the issue."

"It doesn't matter now. But let's not ruin your day with such talk."

Philip felt someone tap his shoulder just then. He looked up to find Miss Millicent smiling down at him. "Excuse me, dear boy, but you two were so engrossed in your conversation that I hesitated to intrude. We are all preparing to leave for the wedding. Perhaps you would like to join us."

Glancing around the empty dining room, Philip saw Henry standing in the doorway, his pocket watch in his hand.

"Sorry, son," he said with an abashed grin, "but it would seem the height of bad form if the groom were late for his own wedding."

At one o'clock, the Creighton entourage arrived at the Stockton home. In the entry hall, Philip took Jessica aside and asked her to take a gift up to Elizabeth.

"I'd be happy to," Jessica said, eyeing the beautifully wrapped box. Then her eyes grew cloudy. Throwing herself into his arms, she cried, "Oh, Philip, I'm going to miss you so much."

"Don't take on so, Jessie. I will be living just a few blocks away."

"I know, but it won't be the same," she sniffed. "Nothing ever stays the same."

"We would stagnate if nothing changed. Now hurry along, little sister. I want to see my gift on my bride when she walks down the aisle." He turned to speak to Henry and Ursula but found that they had already accompanied Mary Stockton outside to greet their guests.

Out on the lawn, Philip mingled with the guests that included the governor, the senator, and the mayor of Crossroads. He saw Ursula chatting with Mary Stockton and the mayor's wife while casting her ever-critical eye first at the threatening sky, then at the decor.

Ferns and white roses trailed in profusion from the arch where Philip and Elizabeth would exchange their vows. The table bearing the wedding cake was banked by vases of cascading white roses and palm leaves, while fronds of delicate ferns bordered each of the guest tables covered with white damask. The silver candelabra and punch bowl gleamed despite the glowering clouds that threatened to open up at any moment and ruin the joyous occasion.

Promptly at one-thirty, the string quartet intoned the traditional wedding music and the service began. Philip and Matthew took their places at the flowered arch, awaiting the bride's arrival. Jessica, as the sole bride's maid, preceded a radiant Elizabeth down the canvas-covered aisle. Her white silk gown, custom-made by the best dressmaker in

Philadelphia, featured the fullest hoop skirt anyone had ever seen. It was adorned with seed pearls and tiny satin rosettes on hand-worked lace.

Displayed proudly around her neck was Philip's gift--a strand of perfectly matched pearls with a diamond clasp.

At the flowered arch, Arthur Stockton handed the bride over to Philip, who eagerly grasped her hand and turned toward Reverend Bates. During the exchange of vows, Philip repeated his vows in a strong, clear voice. Elizabeth responded in a maidenly, almost hesitant voice barely heard beyond the second row of folding chairs. Keeping her eyes lowered, she blushed modestly as Philip slipped the gold ring on her finger.

After the exchange of vows, the bride and groom sat for the photographer who recorded this momentous occasion. On cue from Arthur, the musicians began playing as the caterer served the champagne and hors d'oeuvres.

Once they had completed the obligatory receiving line, Philip took Elizabeth's hand. "May I claim the first dance, Mrs. Creighton?"

She blushed in a most becoming manner and curtsied. "Of course, Mr. Creighton."

As they swirled around the dance platform, he whispered against the veil surrounding her face, "Happy, Mrs. Creighton?"

"Oh, Philip, I can't tell you how happy I am that this day has finally arrived."

"I have another surprise for you." He smiled as she cocked her head to indicate interest.

"I have engaged an architect and a contractor to build us a house on the knoll at the far end of Center Street. They have already begun construction."

"What a wonderful surprise, darling," she cooed. "Thank you, thank you. I can't wait to decorate it. I intend that everyone in town shall be jealous of my--our new mansion."

Julian strolled among the guests, champagne glass in hand. He socialized with the governor, made the mayor's wife blush at his profuse compliments, and promised a dance to every young lady in sight.

Occasionally stealing a glance in the direction of the happy bride and groom, he chuckled to himself.

Later, he approached Philip and lifted his champagne glass. "Congratulations, old man. If I may, I would like your permission to dance with your lovely bride."

"Of course." Philip flashed a confident smile that never quite reached his eyes.

Julian offered his arm to Elizabeth. "May I, cousin Elizabeth?"

With the music and laughter to drown out their conversation, Elizabeth whispered, "Are you mad, asking me to dance after what happened last month?"

"Don't fret, my dear. Philip wouldn't dare make a scene over something as innocuous as my asking my cousin to dance. Besides, my curiosity has gotten the better of me about the story you concocted for Philip's benefit after our, uh, little scuffle. I'll wager it was a classic."

"Yes, it was." Her eyes darkened. "However, I must admit that I cried for two days after we got home, fearful of what he might do. When he did visit me, he was cold and distant, and said he was ready to release me from our betrothal." She flashed a smile at a couple dancing by.

"But I couldn't let that happen, could I?" she continued, her eyes narrowed. "So I gave the performance of my life with the most convincing tears you have ever seen. But they were truly tears of desperation. I assured him that I wanted to marry no one but him. Which is true, of course. When I finished fawning over him, he couldn't keep his hands off me."

"You are a lovely little witch," Julian chuckled. "My life, on the other hand, has not been quite as exciting. I did accomplish one thing, however. You remember that slave wench Mandy who said those nasty things about me during that altercation with Philip? Well, I gave her a beating she won't soon forget. Then I sold her to a former classmate in Virginia."

Elizabeth's eyes widened. "You sold her?"

"Of course. I couldn't have that nigger bitch holding something like that over my head. Got a good price for her too, and kept the money," he added with a smug grin. "I paid off a few debts, enjoyed a few women, and bought some new clothes."

"What did you tell your father?"

"I convinced him that she had stolen from me, and that it wasn't the first time. I'm not sure he believed me but," Julian shrugged, "he didn't contradict me either."

"Oh, Julian," she laughed, "you are incorrigible."

"Yes," he smiled down at her. "We make quite a pair, don't we?"

When the dance ended, Julian escorted her back to Philip and bowed ever so slightly. "Thank you, Philip. I wish you both every happiness."

Philip's smile remained frozen in place, but he did not respond.

Elizabeth linked her arm through Philip's. "I have no doubt that we will be very happy. Thank you for the dance, Julian."

"Cousin Elizabeth," Julian murmured, and strolled away, still chuckling.

After muttering and grinding his teeth for nearly an hour, Arthur Stockton came to a decision. Taking time out from his duties as host, he approached Elizabeth and bowed with great ceremony. "May I claim one last dance from my little girl?"

"Of course, Papa. Excuse me, please," she said to the mayor.

Once they were dancing out of earshot of the others, Arthur hissed, "Have you lost your mind? If you think I missed those looks passing between you and Philip's roguish cousin, you're sadly mistaken. I do not trust that slick-tongued rascal. He is too smooth, his words mendacious. And to make matters worse, I overheard some gossip during the receiving line about that scoundrel's unsavory reputation with the ladies."

"What has that to do with me?" she asked with wide, innocent eyes.

"I warned you that I will not have you jeopardizing everything we have worked so long and hard to achieve. Do I make myself clear?" he growled.

"Don't worry, Papa," she assured him with a smile. "All I did was dance with Julian. With Philip's permission, I might add."

"Permission be damned. I'm warning you, Miss, behave yourself or all will be lost."

"Oh, very well," she pouted. "I will act like a good little wife. But it is only fair to warn you that I will not have anyone telling me how to act after today."

"Now that the deed is done, you may do as you damn well please with whomever you please. So long as you are discreet," he added significantly.

"Yes, Papa." She curtsied at the end of the dance. "I will be a good little girl."

Chapter 12

AFTER WAVING GOOD-BYE to their last guests, Mary and Jessica helped Elizabeth change into her traveling dress. On her way to join Philip, Elizabeth gushed over her new family. "Oh, Maggie, I can't tell you how much I enjoyed my visit last month. I trust all is going well with you and Peter Mitchell."

Returning the embrace, Maggie blushed. "Yes," she whispered into Elizabeth's ear. "He has even asked Father's permission to call on me."

"How wonderful for you." Turning, Elizabeth beamed at Helen and Benjamin. "You must promise to visit Philip and me at the first opportunity. Julian," she said formally, offering her hand, "thank you for coming today."

"Believe me, it was my pleasure, cousin Elizabeth," he responded with a knowing grin.

Returning the pressure of Julian's fingers, she smiled at Jessica and thanked her for being her Maid of Honor. After a quick hug, she slipped a small gift into Jessica's hand.

"Mrs. Creighton," Elizabeth embraced Ursula with unusual warmth, "may I call upon you for help at first? I want to do everything just right for Philip."

"Of course, dear. Feel free to call on me at any time. But I insist that you call me Mother. After all, we are family now."

"Thank you, Mrs.--" she blushed and stammered, "excuse me--Mother Creighton."

Philip appeared at the front door, looking anxious. "My dear Mrs. Creighton, your carriage awaits."

"Coming, Philip. Well," she said, casting one last look of maidenly fear at the group, "as Philip's dutiful wife, I must be away. Thank you all. Good-bye, Mother, Papa," she added with a perfunctory hug for her mother. She and her father exchanged satisfied smiles.

As Philip assisted her into the closed carriage, a bolt of lightning struck nearby followed by the deep rumble of thunder. The storm that had threatened since morning chose this precise moment to break in all its fury.

"Oh, my," Elizabeth cried out, jumping at the sound.

"Did it frighten you?" Philip asked, laughing and shaking raindrops from his hair.

"A little," she said, and snuggled against him.

Philip slid his arm around her and drew her close. "I see you are wearing my wedding gift."

"Oh, Philip, I adore my pearls. How generous and sweet you are. Thank you."

He kissed her fingers. "You are quite welcome."

Turning innocent, yellow-flecked eyes on him, she said, "You cannot imagine how I feel at this moment."

In their suite at the Strand Hotel, Elizabeth gave her gushing approval to their luxurious accommodations. She eyed the fresh flowers and baskets of fruit and champagne the hotel had left for them.

"Shall I open the champagne now, Mrs. Creighton?" he inquired as he twirled the bottle in its silver bucket.

"If you like," she responded playfully, and kissed his cheek.

He popped the cork and poured each of them a glass. "What shall we toast?" He gazed at her, his eyes dark with desire.

"To the future, with its endless possibilities," she replied decisively. After sipping her champagne, she put the glass aside and yawned with great affectation. "I'm exhausted. I believe I will ring for the maid."

"I will wait here until you finish changing."

After what seemed a reasonable length of time, Philip entered the bedroom to discover that she hadn't finished changing. Walking around her, he surveyed the endless yards of linen and lace on her chemise and petticoats. "Good lord, what is all this?"

Elizabeth covered her bosom and, turning to the hotel maid, said, "All right, miss, you may go." After the maid left, she turned on Philip, huffing, "This is downright indecent."

"Indecent? As your husband, I have every right to see you in all those silly petticoats. By the way, how many do you have under there?"

She yanked her petticoats away from him. "Your behavior is scandalous."

"My dear wife--and you are my wife--my behavior is perfectly normal." Laughing, he pulled her onto the bed with him. "I have waited all day for this moment." He kissed her tenderly at first then his kisses became more urgent.

"Philip, please," she protested, squirming to break free from his embrace.

He chuckled against her throat. "No need to beg, my dear. I intend to do my duty."

She jerked free and sat up. "Really, Philip, I thought you would be more considerate. I have a vicious headache from all the fuss today, and too much champagne." She turned toward him, her eyes lowered, her chin quivering. "I hope you understand what I mean," she whined.

Philip rolled away from her. What luck, he sighed. A tired wife with a headache on my wedding night. Or, he thought with a sinking feeling, maybe she meant something else. No, it can't be the wrong time of the month for her. I wonder how many other men have found themselves in this predicament.

"I understand," he said, patting her hand. "I won't distress you tonight."

"Thank you, Philip. I knew you would understand." After a noncommittal embrace, she turned over and didn't move the rest of the night.

Restless and frustrated, Philip slipped out of bed to the sitting room and drank the last of the champagne that had already gone flat. He stretched out on the sofa, with his hands clasped behind his head, and wondered if Elizabeth's reticence to make love tonight may have had something to do with Julian.

That's foolish, he decided. We already settled that issue. I must stop seeing goblins where there are none. Her reticence can only be attributed to nerves and youthful inexperience.

Or that damned female thing.

Chapter 13

NEXT DAY, ON the train ride to New York City, neither Philip nor Elizabeth mentioned the previous night's incident. Nor did she question why he'd slept on the sitting room sofa.

Upon arriving at the luxurious St. Nicholas Hotel on Broadway, Elizabeth was overwhelmed by its frescoed ceilings and walnut wainscoting. "Oh, Philip, have you ever seen anything like it in your life? Look at the gas chandeliers. We must have some for our new house."

Philip smiled at the wonder in her eyes. "Yes, we will order them before we leave."

The following week, they traveled to Saratoga for the horse races where Elizabeth lost several hundred dollars, but Philip simply shrugged it off. Then, to his surprise, she begged him to return to New York City. Smiling at her breathless foray into the world of wealth and privilege, he continued indulging her every whim.

Believing he'd allowed Elizabeth sufficient time to recover from her female problem, Philip decided to approach her again, only more subtly this time. To create a romantic atmosphere, he ordered a dinner of lobster and champagne brought to their suite. Fresh flowers and her favorite chocolates adorned the table.

"Oh, pooh," she pouted, looking at the inviting table flickering in the candlelight, "I had my heart set on going to Delmonico's again."

"We can go to Delmonico's tomorrow evening," he said, leading her to the table. After they were seated, he handed her the flowers. "I thought you might like these."

"Thank you, darling. They are lovely." As she devoured the lobster dinner, Elizabeth made light conversation, and even laughed at Philip's attempts at humor.

At the end of the meal, he filled her glass with the last of the champagne. "Isn't this more intimate than the crowd at Delmonico's?" he asked, his voice suggestive of his intent.

"Not that again." At his wounded look, she bit her lip and hastened to say, "Oh, Philip, I'm so sorry. It was a selfish thing to say. Please forgive me."

"I understand your reticence, sweetheart, but I see no reason for further delay."

Picking her up with a flourish, he carried her to the bedroom and placed her gently on the bed. He kissed her while loosening her dress. She didn't resist when his breathing became more rapid, his lips insistent. Nor did she move.

Just as he freed her of the last encumbrance, she pulled away from him and sat up, crying, "No, please, stop. I can't do this."

Philip fell back onto the pillow with an exasperated sigh. "Don't fret, sweetheart. It is only natural that you would be afraid at first."

"Oh, Philip, I am afraid," she said in a quivering voice. "Mother didn't tell me about, well, anything."

He placed a tentative hand on her shoulder. "I would never force myself on you. Come here, Let me hold you. Everything will be all right."

She lay in his arms, silent and satisfied.

Late the next afternoon, as Philip was getting shaved and groomed at Phalon's Hair-Dressing Establishment for men next to the hotel,

Elizabeth paced back and forth in their suite. 'Control, daughter,' Arthur's voice rang in her ears. 'That's what it is all about. Control.'

"Yes, control," she muttered, and threw herself onto the bed. Papa expects me to consummate this joke of a marriage so everything will be nice and legal. I can do this. I must do it. Sitting up, she said aloud, "I have fooled Philip so far, I can fool him with this too. It might even be fun leading him on."

When Philip returned at four o'clock, he found Elizabeth in the bedroom. Throwing his jacket onto the back of a chair, he said, "Remember, we have been invited to the home of Mr. and Mrs. Garrett this evening. It promises to be a glittering affair, so wear one of those Worth gowns you bought last week."

Elizabeth turned to greet him with a smile and a negligee draped open to reveal her décolletage. "What time are they expecting us?"

Taken back by her seductive appearance, he stammered, "Uh, eight o'clock. Are you all right?" he asked with a confused frown.

"Do I look all right?" she asked, twirling about for his benefit.

"You look delicious."

"Well then, eight o'clock should give us sufficient time," she said, and let the peignoir drop from her shoulders. "Wouldn't you say?"

Smiling, he loosened his cravat and turned down the lamp. "More than sufficient time."

At ten minutes past eight, their cab pulled up to the carriage block in front of the Garrett home. Elizabeth tapped Philip's arm with her fan. "Wipe that satisfied smile off your face. Everyone will guess why we are late."

"Let them," he grinned, as he handed her down from the cab. "The men will be envious of me, and the ladies will be jealous, especially when they see how gorgeous you look in that gown. Even if it does reveal a bit too much," he added with a glance at her décolletage.

Laughing, they entered the Garrett home arm in arm.

Preston Garrett came forward to greet them. "Ah, there you are, Creighton. We were beginning to worry."

"We were unavoidably delayed," he replied with a suppressed grin. "I would like to present my wife, Elizabeth. My dear, this is our host, Preston Garrett."

"Mr. Garrett," Elizabeth murmured, and offered her gloved hand.

Mr. Garrett raked an appreciative eye over her voluptuous body. "My very dear Mrs. Creighton. Come along," he said, offering his arm to her. "I will introduce you to the others."

After meeting their hostess Minerva Garrett, Philip and Elizabeth were presented to the other guests. Philip talked with a banker who, while lobbying for the Creighton business, kept a lustful eye on Elizabeth. Smiling to himself, Philip watched as she tried not to gawk too blatantly at the flashing wealth and glittering jewels. He realized that, having grown up with privilege and wealth, he had always been on the inside. Elizabeth, on the other hand, had always had her nose pressed against the glass of all those things just beyond her reach.

Tonight, however, with her golden hair piled high to show off her graceful neck, she held her own against the matrons who dripped diamonds and old money.

Philip was still admiring her when a familiar voice behind him said, "Hello, Creighton."

Grimacing, he turned to face what he'd feared since arriving in New York. "Good evening, Senator Tate. How are you?"

"Quite well, thank you."

Philip cleared his throat. "And Samantha?"

The Senator's eyes clouded. "As well as can be expected. She is visiting her cousins at the Jersey shore. After that, she is going on to Washington. She usually sees that my house is ready before Congress returns to work. I remained behind for some personal business. I didn't realize you were in town."

Flushing, Philip breathed an inward sigh of relief to learn that he'd been spared a chance encounter with Samantha. "I am here on my wedding trip," he answered in a hoarse voice.

"Oh?" Senator Tate raised an eyebrow. "Is your wife with you this evening?"

"Yes, sir. That is she in the blue gown." He gestured toward the center of attention.

Senator Tate studied Elizabeth for a moment. "Hmm. Quite lovely. And so young."

Before Philip could utter a non-committal reply, Mrs. Garrett called the guests to dinner.

Laughing and chatting, the guests made their way into the dining room where the table was set for sixteen guests. During their sumptuous meal of oysters, smoked salmon and chocolate mousse, Elizabeth artfully drew attention to herself. She laughed at the compliments paid her by the fawning gentlemen and ignored the pointed silence of the ladies.

Philip spent the entire dinner alternately smiling his appreciation of Elizabeth's triumph and avoiding Senator Jared Tate's eyes.

Chapter 14

PHILIP AWOKE THE next morning to the sweet memories of his first two sexual encounters with Elizabeth--the first one before the Garrett party and again afterward. Smiling, he recalled her eager participation in their lovemaking, which he found surprising. He'd always believed that well-bred young ladies didn't enjoy carnal pursuits. But, he decided with a smug grin, she has put that myth to rest. For someone so inexperienced, she certainly was adept at pleasing him.

Her lips pressing against his ear broke into his drowsy thoughts. "Wake up, lazy bones. I've ordered breakfast. It will be here momentarily."

"After last night," he said with a yawn and a long stretch, "I haven't the strength to eat. I may stay in bed all day."

"With or without me?" she asked, arching an eyebrow.

"What good would the bed be without you?" He sat up abruptly and said with mock authority, "Madam, I will have my breakfast served in bed, followed by more of--"

"Now, now," Elizabeth shook a finger at him, "I fear you will become a satyr."

"I pray the gods would so bless me."

A knock at the door interrupted their playfulness. "Shall I get it?" she asked in a whisper.

"At this moment, I am in no condition to answer anything but the call of nature," he called as he hurried off to the bathroom.

When he returned, his breakfast tray--and his bride--awaited him on the bed. After polishing off their meal and setting aside their trays, the newlyweds lounged against the pillows, enjoying a leisurely cup of coffee and quiet talk.

Elizabeth snuggled against Philip with her ear against his chest. "I can hear your heart beating."

"I'm surprised it isn't racing wildly."

"Are you happy, Philip?"

"Deliriously. What about you? Have your fears been dispelled?"

"Yes," she answered, staring at her diamond ring. "I cannot imagine why I was so afraid."

"Fear of the unknown, I suppose. Anyway, I am glad it's in the past. For both our sakes," he added, and kissed her forehead.

"Philip, dear, would you mind if I asked you something?"

"Of course not, sweetheart. What is it?"

"Well," she said, twisting the corner of the sheet, "as you know, I came to you without a proper dowry. Now, before you say anything, I know that sort of thing means nothing to you but it does to me. When we begin entertaining in our new mansion, I want to do it in grand style. At the moment, I have no china, or silver, linens. Nothing. Would you mind if we purchased those things here in New York?"

"I have a better idea. Why don't we go shopping this afternoon? I saw some fashionable shops up the block. We can look at some furniture too."

Frowning, she bit her lip. "There is one more thing. As you know, getting dressed has become nearly impossible for me. While you are a dear to assist me, you will have to agree that you are all thumbs," she added with a laugh.

"Sorry," he shrugged with a sheepish grin, "I know nothing about women's frills and such."

Elizabeth sat up and twisted around on the bed to face him. "To solve that dilemma, why don't I hire a personal maid?"

"Of course. I should have thought of it myself. I'll ask the hotel for the name of a reputable agency."

"Thank you, Philip. You are a dear," she gushed, and threw herself into his arms.

"I suppose you will want to visit Worth's again."

"Of course." She planted a kiss on his scruffy cheek. "I need so many more things, like slippers, evening gloves and, oh, I can't think of them all now."

"I was afraid of that," he laughed, and allowed her to show her gratitude.

Philip entered their suite the next afternoon to find Elizabeth staring out the window. "Am I interrupting something important?"

She turned toward him with her most charming smile. "No. I'm just a little tired after interviewing all those girls."

"Are you pleased with your selection?"

"Yes. Sally seems perfect. Oh, Philip, I never knew life could be so much fun. What would you say to our buying a house here in New York?"

"My business interests are in Pennsylvania," he countered, as thoughts of trying to avoid Samantha flitted through his brain. "Don't look so disappointed, my dear. If you really have your heart set on it, we can lease an apartment from time to time. Anyway, it is something to consider," he said, putting his arms around her.

"Oh, Philip, you are the sweetest husband any girl could ever have. No man could have been more understanding about, well, you know," she stammered, and blinked back opportune tears. "I cannot imagine what you must think of me."

"I think you are a sweet, innocent young lady and I value you all the more for it. Here, dry your eyes," he said, handing her his kerchief, "and look at what I brought you." He opened the signature blue box from Tiffany's.

At the sight of an ornate diamond lapel watch cradled in blue velvet, her eyes sparkled. "It's lovely. And so many diamonds." She thanked him with an ardent kiss.

He pulled her onto the bed where she continued expressing her gratitude. After a while, he caught his breath and said, "I will have to remember to give you something every day if you are going to respond like this."

"I'm willing if you are," she smiled back at him.

"I will remember that. Now tell me, my dear, what would you like to do next? In the past three weeks, we have seen every show in every theater, been to all the best restaurants, shopped at every shop up and down Broadway, and been invited to the most elegant gatherings. We have been to Saratoga where," he bent a significant look on her, "I lost a great deal of money at the races. What can be left?"

Her face lit up. "I read about a place that sounds interesting." She ran to the sitting room and returned a moment later, carrying a newspaper. She sat on the edge of the bed beside Philip and rifled through the pages. "I saw an advertisement yesterday. Look at this. Why don't we try one of those fashionable Virginia spas, like White Sulphur Springs or Berkeley Springs? Oh, yes, Philip, let's go to Berkeley Springs."

Smiling, he threw up his hands. "How can I resist? Of course, we'll go, even if it is nearly the end of the season."

"It will be great fun," she called over her shoulder as she rang for Sally to help her pack. "And we will be seen by all the best people. I read that President Washington had a summer cottage there."

"Well," Philip chuckled, "if it's good enough for President Washington, it is good enough for the Creightons. The New York merchants, however, will be heartbroken at our departure."

Chapter 15

THE CREIGHTONS SET out for Virginia with their mountain of trunks, hat boxes and Sally, the maid Elizabeth had hired in New York. Arriving in the town of Bath, Virginia, on one of the four daily trains, they found the depot bustling with new arrivals and those departing from their restful taking of the waters.

Caught up in the excitement, Elizabeth said with wonder, "Oh, Philip, there are so many fashionable people here. And the scenery. It's glorious! Aren't you happy we came?"

He was mildly surprised by her reaction to this restful little spa that was a far cry from the elegance and bustle of New York. He merely nodded and helped her into the coach sent by Mr. Strother's Pavilion Hotel. Sally and their luggage followed in the hotel baggage wagon.

They spent their first evening getting acquainted with the resort. "How grand," Elizabeth sighed. "The concierge said we have a choice of so many activities, like croquet and horseback riding. You can go bowling or visit the billiard parlor."

"Yes," Philip nodded. "I noticed that there is a telegraph office in the hotel so I can stay in contact with my office or the newspaper."

Their second day began by drinking several glasses of the obligatory before-breakfast water, she from the Ladies' Spring and he from the Gentlemen's Spring. Elizabeth scheduled them for riding later that morning, bathing in the Roman baths in the afternoon, promenade at five o'clock, dinner at eight, then gambling in the casino.

Philip threw up his hands in exasperation. "How can I keep up this pace? If I go into the baths, I will surely drown."

"You are such an old fuddy-duddy," she teased. "Tomorrow, I have scheduled you for a swim in the gentlemen's pool then we have to meet--"

"Enough. Can't we just read or take walks in The Grove?"

"We can walk during the Promenade where we will be seen," she called as she vanished into her dressing room.

Philip sighed. Would she never run out of energy?

"There you are," Elizabeth said, coming into the hotel lobby the afternoon of their third day at the spa. "I have been looking for you."

"I was in the smoking room," Philip replied, as he kissed her cheek. "What do you need?"

"I am on my way to the ladies writing room. I must send a note to Mother and tell her about all the fun I am having. After that, I have an appointment at the hairdresser. I shouldn't be long."

"Take your time. I plan to do absolutely nothing this afternoon but read."

"With my hair all done up, I will want to go to the casino this evening."

"Whatever makes you happy," he smiled. "I will meet you back in our suite."

Elizabeth nodded agreement. In turning away from him, she bumped into another hotel patron. "I'm sorry," she mumbled, and continued on her way.

Philip had already started toward the gentlemen's reading room when he heard a voice call out his name. He groaned inwardly, *No, it can't be. Not here. Not now.*

Turning slowly, he blanched at the sight of her, her eyes wide in disbelief, clutching her reticule. "Hello, Samantha."

"Are you here alone or with your family?" she asked in a soft voice.

He swallowed hard and managed to mumble, despite his suddenly dry mouth, "I am here with my--wife."

Samantha turned to watch Elizabeth stroll toward the writing room. "That must be the lady who bumped into me." With a pained expression, she took a deep breath before saying, "She is very lovely. Have you been married long?"

Grimacing at her wounded reaction, he said, "No." After an awkward moment, he cleared his throat. "I--uh, I ran into your father last week in New York. He told me you were vacationing with your cousins then you were going on to Washington. I never dreamed I would find you here, of all places."

"I arrived last night with several friends who prevailed upon me to accompany them here to escape the awful heat in Washington. Like you, I never dreamed..." Her voice trailed off. Glancing beyond Philip's shoulder, she stammered, "Well," and turned to leave.

"Samantha, wait." He touched her arm. "We need to talk. Please, don't put me off. There are so many questions I need to ask you."

She gave him a quizzical look before nodding hesitantly.

He led her outside toward The Grove, where couples usually went to avoid being seen. "We can talk in here." Choosing a secluded spot, they sat on opposite ends of a bench.

After an awkward silence, he leaned closer and asked in a hoarse whisper, "What happened? Why did you leave so suddenly?" He started to reach for her hand but thought better of it.

Samantha gazed down at her lap where she had knotted her handkerchief into a ball. "As I said in my note, I realized there would have been no future for us."

"How can you say that?" He inched closer to her on the bench. "We were making plans."

"Yes, your mother told me about your plans," she nodded, choking back tears.

He gave her a puzzled look. "My mother?"

"She was too much of a lady to come right out and say it, but I understood her meaning quite clearly--that you would be discreet in your arrangements with me. I wasn't prepared for that. I had the mistaken impression that you planned to marry me."

"Mistaken impression?" he repeated in an incredulous tone. "My God, I wanted desperately to marry you."

"What about my religion? Or that I had been married before? I can appreciate your mother's view that you must be selective about the woman you marry. After all," she raised a shoulder in a helpless gesture, "what could I have brought to our marriage except scandal and division?"

"And love," he added softly. "You know how deeply I loved you, Samantha." He sat back and stared straight ahead but saw nothing of the tiger lilies blooming in the dappled sunlight. Nor did he hear the birds chattering overhead in the canopy of trees.

"After all that had happened in my past," she offered in a whisper, "I couldn't allow myself to be used again--as your mistress."

Philip turned an incredulous gaze on her. "My mistress? That's ridiculous."

Realizing he'd raised his voice, he took a deep breath before asking with urgency, "Are you saying my mother insinuated that I had less than honorable intentions in mind?"

"I don't think I misunderstood her." She turned to face him, raw fear in her eyes. "Dear God, could I have misunderstood her?"

Philip recalled the day he showed Samantha's note to Ursula. Mother said she found the note confusing and mysterious. Mother said she was greatly concerned for his well being. Mother said.

Mother said.

"No," he said with a bitter edge in his voice and thought, it was I who misunderstood her. And misjudged her. I knew of her opposition to Samantha but never dreamed she would stoop to lies and deception. A new and terrible fury rose within him and began to simmer.

There, in the green seclusion of The Grove, they regarded one another in silence--and remembered.

"I don't know what to say," he said at last in a strangled voice.

Samantha dabbed at her eyes with the wrinkled handkerchief. "I'm so sorry, Philip. I only wanted to do what was right."

"After you left, I was desperate for answers so I wrote to you, seeking an explanation." He paused. "What's wrong? Why are you looking at me that way?"

"I received no such letter from you."

He slumped against the back of the bench. "No, it can't be," he muttered.

"If I had received a letter from you, I would have answered it in the next post."

Jumping to his feet, Philip stormed around in a circle in front of the bench. He raked his fingers through his hair, tousling it even further. Furious, troubling thoughts whirled around in his brain, thoughts and conclusions he dared not voice aloud. *Mother must have seen my letter to Samantha and confiscated it. Her motive was clear. She didn't want Samantha answering any questions. Damn it. I made it perfectly clear to Mother that none of her prejudices or concerns were an issue with me. But meddling into my personal life to this extent is unconscionable.*

He stopped dead in his tracks. *By God, I will not let this pass unchallenged. She will answer for her actions.*

Samantha rose from the bench and stood at his side, watching as he pondered this latest revelation. When he turned to face her, his expression was forlorn. He looked into her eyes, those beautiful green eyes that even now caused his heart to skip a beat. *Oh, Lord*, he groaned deep within himself, *what has Mother done to me? To us?*

"As much as I am loath to admit it," he whispered, "I have reason to suspect that my mother may have intercepted my letter."

She stumbled backward with a small cry. "It's my fault. I should never have left without giving you the opportunity of speaking for yourself. Oh, Philip, please forgive me. I knew how she felt about me, but I never suspected…"

Philip gripped her shoulders. "Don't blame yourself. Don't even think it. You are the innocent victim here. And I was a stupid fool for not following you to New York and setting the matter straight. I let my foolish pride blind me. No, the blame lies elsewhere."

They stood close together, gazing into each other's eyes. Suddenly, all was stillness. Nothing existed outside the immediate space surrounding them. Philip could feel heat prickling under his collar but his hands felt cold. He did not release his hold on her, nor did she attempt to move.

Memories of her kisses flooded over him. He gazed at her lips. He wanted to kiss her even though his bride was only a few hundred yards away. He fought the urge to take Samantha by the hand, run far away from this place and never look back. But he knew what her reply would be to such a scandalous suggestion.

As she leaned closer, he felt her trembling under his touch. "Samantha, what are we to do? I love you as much today as I ever have."

Samantha reached up and caressed his face. "My feelings for you have not changed either. I will always love you. But what can we do? It is too late for us. The only sensible recourse is for me to take the next train to Washington. It would be too awkward and painful if I stayed."

Grabbing her wrist, he held it fast. "Will I see you again?"

"Oh, Philip, what good would it do? You are married to a lovely young girl with no scandal attached to her name." She exhaled a sigh devoid of all hope. "There is nothing we can do about it. Things must remain as they are."

Their faces were just inches apart when he whispered, "The memory of what we had will haunt me for a very long time."

Slowly, reluctantly, Samantha withdrew her hand from his and retrieved her reticule from the bench. "Good-bye, Philip. I wish you happiness." She hurried away before he could reply.

Philip stood in The Grove for a long time, oblivious to the other couples strolling by. He saw nothing through his blurred vision except Samantha's retreating figure. Oh, Mother, he thought, if you only knew what you have cost me.

"Damn!" he swore aloud suddenly, and rammed his fist against the trunk of the nearest Sycamore tree, pounding it until his knuckles bled.

Chapter 16

ELIZABETH RETURNED TO their suite shortly after five o'clock to find Sally and two hotel maids packing their trunks. "Where is Mr. Creighton?" she asked, glancing around at the activity.

Sally pointed toward the bathroom. "In there, ma'am."

Puzzled, Elizabeth knocked on the bathroom door and called out. She waited until he bade her to enter. When she opened the door, she saw Philip reclining in a tub, holding a glass in one hand and a bottle of bourbon in the other.

"Why are you in the tub at this time of day?"

"I needed a bath," he said, between sips of bourbon. "I suddenly felt--dirty."

"You look strange," she said, closing and locking the door behind her. At the sight of bloodied knuckles on his right hand clutching the bottle, she asked, "What happened to your hand? It looks as though it's been bleeding. Did you have an accident?"

He studied his raw knuckles as though seeing them for the first time. "An accident? No, it wasn't an accident," he answered, slurring his words. "Nothing is an accident. Hand me that towel." Standing, he stepped unsteadily from the tub, dripping bath water onto the floor. He took the towel Elizabeth held out for him and vigorously dried his hair.

Elizabeth eyed him warily, recalling that she'd never seen him drunk before. And he seemed to have changed in the two hours since she left him in the lobby. What could have happened to bring about this unexpected change? Does he suspect something? How could he?

"Philip, dear," she asked, her voice tentative, "why are the maids packing our things?"

"We are taking the next train to Crossroads," he replied in a detached voice as he tossed the towel aside. "Some urgent business has arisen that requires my immediate attention."

Philip and Elizabeth returned to Crossroads five weeks after their wedding with far more luggage than when they departed. Arriving at home just before midnight, they saw their trunks deposited in the entry hall then went directly to bed, with Philip's assurance that he would take her the first thing in the morning to see how her mansion was progressing.

As promised, Philip and his bride stood on the windswept knoll where the sun had already made its way above the treetops. Glowing with pride, Elizabeth hugged her arms around herself and cooed, "Oh, Philip, what a beautiful spot. I can look down on the whole town from here."

He regarded her with a wry smile, thinking, yes, everyone's dream of conquest. He turned his attention to the mansion's skeletal framing. "This property is part of my inheritance from my grandfather Jasper Creighton. I always viewed it as the perfect spot for my future wife and family." Recalling his plans for Samantha, he grew angry which only strengthened his resolve for the task ahead.

He grasped Elizabeth by the elbow and said in terse tone that surprised her, "Come along, dear. You must see to the unpacking of the crates from New York while I attend to something."

Fifteen minutes later, the maid Jenny announced Philip's arrival to Ursula.

Descending the stairs, Ursula greeted him with a smile. "Philip, dear, I didn't expect you and Elizabeth until later this week." She opened her arms to embrace him but he backed away from her, avoiding all contact. "You look pale, son. Are you unwell?"

"As a matter of fact, I feel like hell. Don't gasp, Mother. I am in no mood for niceties. I must speak with you about something."

"I'm sorry. I haven't much time," she huffed, and reached for her reticule. "I was just about to leave for a meeting."

"This will only take a few minutes," he said, ushering her into the parlor. He slid the doors closed behind them and turned to face her.

After she'd taken a seat, she folded her hands over the reticule in her lap. "Very well, what is so important? My hospital committee is waiting for me."

"Everyone waits on you, don't they? Life revolves around you. The sun, in fact, revolves around you," he remarked, and gestured in a wide arc.

She raised her eyebrows. "I do not appreciate your harsh and unwarranted assessment of my character," she said through pursed lips. "Is there some point to this?"

He savored her obvious discomfort for several seconds before admitting in a deceptively light tone, "Yes. I came to bring you a social note from my travels."

Ursula sat up, alert, her curiosity piqued. "Really?"

Philip nearly laughed out loud at how easily she was distracted by all things social. With a barely concealed edge to his voice, he said, "You will never guess who I met at Berkeley Springs. Someone I am sure you will never forget--Samantha Ryder."

Ursula blinked several times before asking in a quavering voice, "Oh? How--how is she?"

"How would you expect her to be, especially after all those damned lies you told her? Yes," he nodded, in response to Ursula's shocked reaction, "Samantha told me everything you said the day she had tea with you."

Ursula fussed with her gloves. "I don't know what that Ryder woman told you, but she obviously fabricated something to justify her peculiar actions."

"She told me you insinuated in the broadest terms possible that I intended to make her my mistress. You know perfectly well that I had no such thing in mind. Even when I showed you Samantha's note, you swore you had no idea what it meant." His eyes hardened. "You are the only person besides Samantha herself who understood its true meaning."

"No, you are wrong," she stammered, dabbing her handkerchief at the perspiration that glistened on her upper lip. "I told you I didn't understand it."

"How can you expect me to believe you when the facts say otherwise? And another thing," he said, jabbing the air with his index finger, his voice rising to match his full-blown fury, "I do not appreciate your purloining the letter I wrote to Samantha."

Ursula stared at him, her lips compressed into a tight line, but she didn't bother denying it.

"I couldn't understand why Samantha did not reply to my inquiry. Now I do. She never received the damned thing."

Ursula fanned herself with her gloves. "Philip, I have never seen you like this, shouting and swearing like some common--."

"How in the hell do you expect me to act after learning of your unconscionable treachery?" He bent over until he was at eye level with her. "What, I would like to know, gives you the right to meddle in my personal life? Do you have any idea how betrayed and revolted I felt when Samantha told me how you lied about me and my motives? Or that you could even believe I was capable of treating a lady of virtue and character as a trollop?"

They regarded one another at close range for several seconds before he straightened up. It was then he realized that consideration for his--or anyone's--feelings was not part of her make-up. How, he asked himself, could he have been so blind as not to have seen it before?

"What passed between Samantha and me during our brief courtship," he said at last, "is none of your business, but I will tell you that I never laid a hand on her. I have too much respect for her and, more than that, I was sensible of how that bastard of a husband had beaten and raped her, even stolen jewelry and money from her to pay his gambling debts. Knowing all that, how could I have treated her with anything but esteem? I loved her. She made me happy and I wanted her for my wife. But you can't understand love, can you? You are devoid of that emotion."

Rising from her seat with all the majesty of a crowned head, Ursula pulled on her gloves. "I will not tolerate a moment more of this abuse. I am already late for my meeting."

Scowling, he stood before the door, his arms crossed, blocking her exit. "That will have to wait. I have a few more things to say."

He waited until she resumed her seat, the bravado gone from her demeanor. He paced before the closed doors, his head down, considering. He stopped and regarded her, his eyes narrowed. "How, I kept asking myself, had this curious situation come about? Then it came to me. While I was planning my future with Samantha, you were making plans of your own for Elizabeth who, we were given to understand, was descended from a distinguished New England family. I have always been cognizant of your obsession with the purity of the Creighton blood and I am painfully aware of your prejudice against Catholics. But it took me a little longer to grasp your real motive in this matter. After careful reflection, it became clear to me at last."

With a suppressed smile, he saw her stiffen, her gloved hands gripping the arms of the chair.

"You reign here in your own little world as the queen of Crossroads society. As such, you perceived Samantha as an unwanted rival to all that because her blood line is older and more distinguished than ours. She could buy and sell the meager Creighton holdings with a wave of her hand. She owns some of the most valuable real estate in New York City, as well as her Dutch grandmother's Hudson valley estate. Samantha was a threat to your idea of self entitlement," he said, pointing a finger at her. "So she had to go. Never mind how it might affect the lives of others because, above all else, you must prevail."

He ignored her attempt at protest. "I have one more thing to say then I am finished with you." Lowering his voice, he continued with icy intensity, "As a direct result of your perfidy, do not expect me to treat you with the same respect I once accorded you. As of today, you are no longer welcome in my home when I am there. I will be civil to you only when the situation demands it. I will maintain appearances for my benefit, on my terms. Not yours."

In one swift motion, he slid the doors open with a resounding thud. "You are now free to go out into your domain and continue meddling into the affairs of others." He stood aside as she swept past him, her gaze averted, and added, "But you will rue the day you meddled into mine.

Chapter 17

THE SOUND OF Philip's carriage wheels beneath her window awakened Elizabeth the next morning. Smiling, she enjoyed a long, luxurious stretch in the four-poster bed, her plan worked out in great detail during the night.

At that point, Sally entered the room, carrying the breakfast tray. "Good morning, Mrs. Creighton. Mr. Creighton has already left for his office."

"Thank you, Sally. I will be gone most of the day myself. Lay out one of my new outfits. The blue silk afternoon dress, I believe. Oh, and by the way, let me know when Mr. Creighton's driver returns with the carriage."

"Yes, ma'am."

Later that morning, Elizabeth sat in Philip's carriage outside the hardware store while her driver purchased the items necessary to implement her plan. Just before noon, she arrived at her parents' home to cries of joy and welcoming kisses.

"Shouldn't you be at home to receive callers?" Mary asked, dismayed.

Elizabeth waved off her suggestion. "Nonsense, Mother. I will do as I please now."

"But dear, it is expected of someone in your position."

"I am exercising the rights of my position. After all, I am Mrs. Philip Creighton," Elizabeth sniffed with disdain then proceeded to describe all the beautiful things she bought in New York. "Philip can afford to buy me anything I want," she added breathlessly. "And so many other things I didn't even ask for, like this diamond lapel watch."

Mary leaned closer to examine it. "It's breathtaking. Is that a new outfit too?"

Twirling around with a flourish, Elizabeth showed off her dress with muff and matching hat. "Do you like it? I bought so many new dresses and gowns, evening gloves and, oh, so many other things, I can't begin to name them all. And Philip simply has the bills sent to the bank."

"How pretty you look, daughter," Arthur observed with a proud smile. "Every inch the society belle. I hope Philip realizes what a lucky man he is."

Elizabeth recalled Arthur's oft-spoken admonition about the best way to keep Philip dangling and begging for more. Biting her lip, she realized how outraged her father would be if he ever learned of her plan.

Pushing that gloomy thought from her mind, she chatted happily, "We attended the most elegant parties and dinners. Philip knows so many rich men. And their wives." She rolled her eyes. "Goodness, those ugly old cows dripped diamonds and jewels. Philip bragged on and on about how young and beautiful I was."

Arthur smiled his approval. "Tell us about the swells at Saratoga."

"It was so much fun betting on the horses and meeting such fashionable people. Eventually, I became bored with New York, so we went to a spa in Virginia for the waters and the gambling.

All the right people from Washington City vacation there. Some even maintain summer cottages for their families. I believe I'll suggest to Philip that we build a cottage there," she added, after a thoughtful pause. "Yes, that's what we'll do, so everyone will know how important we are."

Mary nodded reserved approval of her daughter's plans before saying, "I understand you had many crates and barrels sent home from New York."

"Oh, Mother, you must see the Gorham silver and Royal Doulton china I bought. Even my esteemed mother-in-law doesn't have china as grand as mine, or silver as ornate. I can't wait to show it off in my new house. Goodness," she said, glancing at her lapel watch, "look at the time. I really must fly. Before I go, I'll need to speak to that Irish fellow who works for you now and then. I have a little chore for him."

Philip and Elizabeth sat down to dinner several days later, using her new table settings and linens for the first time. "Isn't the new silver beautiful in the candlelight?" Elizabeth cooed.

Philip nodded and tried to make conversation, but his mind kept drifting back to his encounter with Samantha. Several times during dinner, he rubbed the knuckles on his wounded hand and his eyes grew cloudy with remembering.

"Philip, I'd like to talk to you about the things that must be done regarding the new house."

Bringing himself back to the moment, he cocked a wary eyebrow. "That sounds expensive."

"Not really," Elizabeth laughed. "People in our position must maintain a certain image. After we move into the new place, we will be entertaining quite a bit, so we will need to increase the household staff. They should have new uniforms instead of the tacky ones the current help are wearing now. Also, we will need someone to design the formal gardens and hire grounds keepers."

Philip threw up his hands and laughed. "I knew it would be expensive. I agree that the house will require a larger staff, but we have several months before making those decisions."

"Why wait?" she pressed. "We need to find suitable people through agencies, and there are the interviews. I also need to see about the furnishings, pick out the furniture and window dressings. Perhaps even order the finer things from New York City or Europe. So, as you can see," she spread her hands, indicating the obvious to him, "there is quite a bit that needs to be done before we move in."

Philip flashed a helpless smile. "This is getting more expensive with every suggestion."

"Nonsense. We have our status to think of. Speaking of status…"

"If you are going to suggest that I hire a valet, save your breath. I told you before that I dislike having someone hovering over me."

"But Philip…"

"No, Elizabeth, I will not be swayed on that issue. As for the rest, you are right, of course. I will give it some thought."

Elizabeth's eyes turned dark. Ever so delicately, she dabbed her napkin at the corners of her lips. "Very well, you think about."

So, without so much as a word to Philip, Elizabeth proceeded to increase their household staff, with an eye to the future in her grand new mansion. After retaining the services of a much sought-after cook, she summarily fired the cook Philip had hired shortly before their wedding, complaining that the woman couldn't concoct the savory dishes she'd tasted in New York.

Each day, after Philip left for his office, she sat in her morning room unmindful of the early autumn beauty on the hillsides outside her window, and interviewed applicants for the various positions. From these hopefuls, she added two more maids. Finding someone to work on the grounds and the carriage house was easily solved when two middle-aged men showed up, asking for work.

Having filled these positions to her satisfaction, Elizabeth decided that the elegant carriage she had secretly ordered demanded not only a matched pair of mares, but a proper driver. After dismissing several unsuitable applicants, her search proved fruitless and she gave up.

For the time being.

On a blustery morning in early November, Mr. Welles, the carriage maker, arrived with the new phaeton Elizabeth had ordered. With many bows and profuse compliments, Mr. Welles led Elizabeth outside to the porte-cochere to view her purchase. Upon seeing it, she declared that she had never seen anything quite so elegant, with its endless array of polished brass fittings, shining black wheels and the soft red leather interior.

She sat in the middle of the plush seat, beaming. "Mr. Welles, I cannot thank you enough for your courteous service and prompt delivery. I am quite pleased with it."

"I am gratified, Mrs. Creighton. This English George the Fourth style is quite a favorite with the fashionable ladies such as yourself. As you can see, it has all the accessories currently in vogue."

As if by magic, his aspect changed from pleased to businesslike. "Now, if I may, there is the small matter of the invoice." He held it tentatively in the air between them.

"Oh that," she said, her eyes darkening as she took it, "I will see that my husband gets this."

Elizabeth presented herself in Philip's office just before noon that same day. "It is such a gloomy day," she said, "that I decided to drop by and see if you would like to take me to lunch."

"You look so fetching, how can I resist the opportunity to show you off?"

Tom Dayton appeared in the doorway behind Elizabeth. "Sorry to bother you, sir, but your tailor is here."

"Show him in." To Elizabeth, he said, "I hope you will be a patient for a few moments."

Swallowing hard, she nodded and retreated to a far corner.

The tailor entered Philip's office, hat in hand. Nodding with a smile in Elizabeth's direction and greeting her, he stood before Philip's desk.

"Good day, Mr. Baldwin," Philip said. "Are my suits ready so soon?"

"No, sir. That is," he stammered, "well, it's about the other matter."

"What other matter?" Philip asked, noticing Elizabeth inching toward the door.

"The uniforms, sir. It's quite a big order."

Philip frowned. "Uniforms?"

"Yes, sir. For the new maids, the cook, and your drivers."

Philip shot Elizabeth a meaningful glance that told her to stay put. "What is the problem, Mr. Baldwin?"

"Well, sir," his eyes also darted in Elizabeth's direction, "I'm not sure I can have them ready when Mrs. Creighton wants them. So I was wondering if you wanted your order first."

Philip rose slowly and answered in a measured voice, "Yes, Mr. Baldwin, I would like my suits first. Don't worry about the uniforms. Take all the time you need with them."

"Thank you, sir," the tailor said with a relieved smile. "And thank you for seeing me on such short notice."

Philip smiled. "Not at all. I am happy we were able to resolve your dilemma. Good day."

After Mr. Baldwin bowed out of the office, Philip fixed his dark eyes on Elizabeth. "Why, pray tell, is Mr. Baldwin making uniforms for people who don't work for me?"

Elizabeth gave him the full benefit of her most persuasive smile. "But they will be working for you soon."

"After our conversation several weeks ago, did you go ahead and hire new people? I told you that I would think about it and let you know."

Elizabeth approached him slowly, looking properly apologetic. "I'm sorry, I didn't mean any harm. I was just so excited about the new house that I could not wait any longer. Oh, Philip, don't be cross with me. I know how busy you are, and besides," she looked up at him through her lashes, "you would have hired them anyway."

Sighing, he relented. "Yes, I suppose I would have. I just don't like finding out about it this way. It makes me feel that you do not respect my wishes."

She slipped her arms around him. "How can you even think that? You just concentrate on building our beautiful new mansion and think how envious people will be when they see it."

"I am not carried away by the envy of others." Feigning a severe countenance, he shook his finger at her. "Now see here, young lady, in the future..."

She kissed him full on the lips and snuggled hard against him. "Yes, sir. I will be very, very good. You'll see."

Chapter 18

THREE DAYS LATER, Sally informed Elizabeth that a man at the back door wished to see her about the chauffeur's position. On Elizabeth's orders, a tall, distinguished-looking black man was shown into the morning room. Well over six feet tall, he had a full head of iron-gray hair, and carried himself with dignity.

In a deep resonant voice, he informed Elizabeth that his name was Ames. "I was born a free man on a Quaker farm east of Harrisburg. My father worked for the owner of the farm and together, they ran a station in the Underground Railroad for runaway slaves. I moved away from the farm and worked as a gentleman's gentleman for a judge in Philadelphia until he passed on."

Impressed by his manners and flawless grammar, Elizabeth knew she had found the perfect driver for herself. She hired Ames on the spot--Philip's orders notwithstanding.

Later that day, Philip arrived at home early, tired, and distracted by the inflammatory war rhetoric and calls for secession from several southern states on the heels of Lincoln's election to the presidency. In the entry hall, he handed his coat and gloves to the maid, and went directly to his study for a drink to soothe his tired brain.

Elizabeth entered a moment later, dressed for dinner and wearing the pearls he had given her as a wedding gift. "May I light your cheroot for you?" she asked with a smile.

"If you like." She bent toward him with a lucifer in hand and treated him to a voluptuous display of décolletage. She wants something, he thought with a grin. "Did anything interesting happen today?" he asked, puffing the cheroot to life.

Her look became evasive. "As a matter of fact, yes. I hired a driver."

Sitting bolt upright in his chair, Philip nearly dropped the cheroot from his gaping mouth. "Why on earth would you want to replace my driver?"

"It was not my intention to replace him. I--I hired a driver of my own."

"Why? My carriage is always at your disposal."

"Yes, I know. And I thank you," she was quick to add in a conciliatory tone. "But your carriage is so old fashioned. I thought that, well, it's time we had a new one, so I ordered a brand new phaeton."

Jumping from his chair, Philip threw his cheroot into the fireplace. "Oh no," he shook his head, "you will have to cancel the order."

"But I have already taken delivery. It is sitting in the carriage house at this very moment."

"Whatever possessed you to do such a thing?"

"In my position, I need a carriage of my own. Besides," she lowered her eyes, "I assumed you wouldn't mind."

"That is not the point. I did not force the issue when you hired all those additional people or ordered new uniforms without my consent or knowledge because I intended to do it anyway. But," he added, bending over into her face to give her the full force of his rising anger, "I prefer to make those decisions on my own."

Leaving her cringing against the back of the sofa, he reached for a fresh cheroot. "How much is all this going to cost me?"

"I really couldn't say." She avoided looking at him directly. "The carriage maker said he would submit his bill at a later date. I assumed that was his standard procedure."

Before Philip could respond, the maid announced that dinner was served. Taking his drink, he followed Elizabeth into the dining room, his jaw muscles flexing.

Once they had been served, they ate quietly for a while, and eyed one another warily.

After taking a sip of wine, Philip asked, "What have you agreed to pay your driver?"

Without looking up from her dish, she responded, "I wasn't quite sure what you paid your driver, so I told him twenty dollars a month."

"Twenty dollars a month? That is three dollars more than I pay my driver. You will have to tell your driver that his salary is being adjusted or he must assume additional duties to earn the rest."

"I will leave that to you," she said, forcing an accommodating smile. "You are much more suited for that sort of thing than I am."

Putting his fork down carefully, Philip said in an icy voice, "No, my dear, you tell him. As I mentioned before, I do not appreciate your over-riding my authority. You take care of running the house and leave these business decisions to me."

Her expression hardened, her eyes darkening with anger. "You make me sound like an empty-headed dolt, incapable of doing anything."

Throwing down her napkin, she ran from the dining room, leaving a startled Philip to wonder what was happening between them.

The following Friday, Philip settled down in his study to look over several news reports the newspaper editor had sent him about reaction to Lincoln's election as President of the United States. Response from the South was predictable--and swift. Damn, Philip thought with a sinking feeling, this whole mess of States' Rights is becoming uglier every day. He wrote a few notes to the editor, and asked to be kept informed of events.

Feeling suddenly drained, Philip put his work aside, stood up and stretched. The strain of enduring Elizabeth's recent coolness toward his romantic overtures had manifested itself in every aching muscle of his body. She had barely spoken to him since their altercation over the phaeton and hiring a driver. *Perhaps it is time to end this emotional standoff*, he decided with a hopeful smile.

Opening the door to their bedroom, he found Elizabeth at her dressing table, brushing her hair. Tenderly, he kissed her shoulders. His lips moved from her shoulders to her neck.

With his lips pressed against her ear, he whispered, "Why don't we do something to repair this unpleasantness between us?" Bending over her from behind, he reached for the sash on her green silk peignoir.

At his touch, he felt her entire body stiffen and she said, "Don't touch me."

"Sweetheart, I realize that you have been upset since the incident over the phaeton but it needn't come to this. As I said, we can make it up tonight. After all, it has been well over a week since--"

"I said, don't touch me," she repeated through clenched teeth. "Not now or ever again." She rose and whirled around to face him, tying the sash tight around her.

He took a step backward, stunned by this sudden transformation in her appearance. *What*, he wondered, *had happened to the nervous, innocent bride who overcame her fears to drive him mad with raw sexual pleasure? Another even more unnerving thought flashed through his mind: Just how innocent was she?*

And now, how can she have transformed herself into this unrecognizable--what? With her hazel eyes flashing yellow in the lamplight, he realized that she looked more like a predator. Yes, a predator about to devour its prey.

"We will simply come to an understanding," she was saying in a cool voice as he stood there transfixed, "and that will be the end of it."

As she started to sweep past him, he caught her by the arm. "No," he said in a harsh tone, "that will not be the end of it. We will talk about it now." Seeing her flinch under the pressure of his grip, he released her. "What is this 'understanding' we must come to? You make it sound as though it were something to be negotiated."

"There is nothing to negotiate."

"At least we agree on that point." Frustrated, Philip paced in front of the fireplace. "I cannot believe that this bizarre response of yours could have been brought on solely by my reaction to your hiring all those people without my knowledge. Or buying the phaeton. Prior to this misunderstanding, you could not have been more loving, or playful. What happened?"

"Let us be clear about one thing, Philip," she said with a cool smile. "I led you to believe what I wanted you to believe. I knew what I was doing at all times."

So, that answers the question about her so-called innocence, he thought. Calming himself, he forced a reasonable tone. "I still think we should talk about this."

"Really, Philip, this is becoming tiresome," Elizabeth countered with an affected sigh.

"Tiresome? I have every right to make love to you."

"There are women who are paid to do that sort of thing. I expect you not to bother me with it again."

"Don't bother you with it? Madam, I do not need your permission. You are mine for the taking."

He swept her up into his arms and threw her onto the bed. Before she could protest, he tossed her peignoir aside, revealing her ivory skin that felt chill to the touch. Throwing his own robe aside, he kissed her wildly, devouring her like someone possessed. Perspiration dampened his hair. His breathing became rapid.

She remained as cold and still as a statue in his arms.

He raised his head and looked into the angry eyes glaring up at him. They regarded one another at close range for several long moments. Finally, he rolled over, dropped onto the pillow and ran a hand over his damp face.

Elizabeth stood up, pulled on her peignoir and strode across the room in a swirl of green silk. At the door, she turned and gave him a measured look. "If you feel the need for a woman, I am sure there are scores of women who would deem it an honor to be bedded by the great Philip Creighton. You might try one of them. Or," she added with a smirk, "Samantha Ryder."

At the mention of Samantha's name, he tore across the room, grabbed her by the shoulders and shook her violently. "Don't you ever dare to speak that name again, especially not in that regard. Get out of here. Out of my sight!" he shouted.

"With pleasure," she said, wrapping her peignoir, and her shredded dignity, around her. "You see, I have already taken care of that eventuality."

Philip leaned against the doorjamb, trembling and perspiring, but her last remark caught his attention. He looked up at her, puzzled. "What?"

"I have already moved my things to another room."

"Another room?" he asked, as he followed her down the hall.

"Yes, to my room." She turned in the doorway to face him with a smug smile.

He put out his hand to prevent her from closing the door in his face. "What do you mean, 'your room'? This is the guest suite."

"Not any longer. It is now my room. I had my things moved in here several days ago to prevent any such unpleasantness from ever occurring again. Or," she added with tight lips, "the possibility of having a child that would ruin my figure and interfere with my social life."

"Of course. How stupid of me. You wouldn't want any children of mine. You probably cry into your pillow every night because it is not Julian in bed with you." He grabbed her arms and shook her again until she cried out. "Don't you?"

"Let me go. You are hurting me." Elizabeth gave one furious wrench, pulling them both out into the dark hallway. "This is how things will be from now on." Turning, she squared her shoulders, walked into her room and slammed the door.

Still panting from exertion, Philip stared at the closed door. Then he heard the sound that put him over the edge--a bolt sliding into place. A violent red haze passed before his eyes, blinding him momentarily. He stared at the locked door knowing that in his present state of rage, he possessed the strength to pull the door from its hinges and the cherry woodwork with it.

Acting on emotion and reflex, Philip put his shoulder to the door and burst it open with one violent thrust. Elizabeth backed into a corner on the far side of her bed, screaming and waving her hands at him. "Stay away. Don't touch me, you brute. Don't come near me!"

"Fear not, madam. I have no intention of putting hands on you. I merely wanted you to know that nothing or no one will keep me from going any place I choose in my own house."

Pushing the splintered door aside, he stalked from the room.

Back in his own room, Philip paced aimlessly, cursing and mumbling to himself. He glanced around the room where, just days before, lace petticoats, silk stockings and kid gloves carelessly tossed aside spoke of the feminine invasion he had so longed for. It was disturbing enough, he thought, to discover that Mother had thwarted my plans to marry Samantha, but this episode with Elizabeth was completely unexpected. I have never seen such a transformation in anyone. What the hell could have caused her to change so drastically in the short span of time since we returned home from our honeymoon? Do I really know this woman?

Emotionally spent, and shaken to the core by these cumulative revelations, he threw himself into a fireside chair with his chin resting on his chest, wondering what had gone wrong between them. Whatever the answer, he concluded with great reluctance, this short-lived marriage appears to be a disaster.

The question is--can it be remedied?

Chapter 19

JANUARY OF 1861 seemed endless, with its dreary days of being snowed in, followed by days of dazzling sun glittering on the snow and icicles that hung heavy from roof lines and the trees. But to Philip, each day had the dull sameness as the day before.

He and Elizabeth still avoided one another following their violent argument and subsequent sleeping arrangements. He buried himself in his work, going from home to the office and back again. He took his meals at the hotel. For her part, Elizabeth disappeared for days at a time, without a word to anyone.

During this two month period, his physical appearance underwent a stark transformation. Gone was the spring in his step. He moved through his days as though in a trance, hollow-eyed and thin, acting on instinct rather than interest in his business dealings. And he exerted every effort to absent himself from home--and any contact with Elizabeth.

Returning from an extended business trip at the end of the month, Philip went directly to his office. No need to hurry home, he mused. I would most likely intrude upon another one of her parties that I didn't know about. After a short meeting with Tom Dayton, Philip caught up on matters requiring his immediate attention then looked over the accumulated mail.

"May I come in?" Henry asked, knocking on his door.

Philip glanced up with a start. "Of course, Pa. Have a seat."

"If you have a moment, son, I would like to speak with you about something that causes me great anxiety."

Philip raised an eyebrow. "And what has caused this state of anxiety?"

"You have. Are you ill, son? I have noticed a significant weight loss on your part, and you had none to spare. This concerns me."

Philip dropped his pen onto his desk, splattering ink across the blotter. "Oh hell, Pa, frankly, I don't know what is wrong. I can't eat. I can't sleep. I find it hard to concentrate."

"Is everything all right at home?"

Philip reached for a cheroot. "Why do you ask that?"

"Because you have changed since your marriage, but not in a way I would have expected."

"Nothing is the way we expect, is it, Pa? I have learned one thing these past few months--there are some people with whom you cannot be generous or considerate. Those qualities are perceived as weakness. Or," he added in a dismal voice, "the means to an end."

Henry settled back in his chair. "Would you care to elaborate?"

Philip gazed at his father long and hard before answering, "It's nothing specific. Just a series of events, beginning with our trip to Uncle Ben's last summer that should have alerted me to several unforeseen issues with Elizabeth."

"Julian."

Philip looked up sharply at his father's keen observation. "You knew?"

"A safe assumption, given Julian's reputation as a scoundrel and womanizer," Henry replied with a shrug. "If you ask me, I think they both showed their true colors during that trip. And, as I recall, I voiced my doubts about your alliance with this girl on several occasions. I recognized a familiar look in Elizabeth's eyes. A look with which I am all too familiar."

"If ever the devil came in a pretty package, it was in Elizabeth." Philip snuffed out his cheroot and said with disgust, "I have been such a damned fool. Love had nothing to do with our marriage from the beginning. For her, it was always about the Creighton name and the money."

"It always is," Henry agreed.

Philip nodded, his eyes now solemn. "But I would never have suspected my own mother of being a part of it." Seeing Henry's lack of reaction, he said, "You don't seem at all surprised."

"I'm not." Henry steepled his fingers and studied them intently. "You see, after your mother and I had been married for several years, she announced that four children more than fulfilled her conjugal obligation. She wanted to be free to preside over the local society, and enjoy watching lesser mortals quake in her imperious presence."

"I--I'm sorry, Pa. What did you do?"

Henry chuckled, but his eyes remained deadly serious. "I handled it by appearing to do nothing. The one thing that has always infuriated your mother was my not responding when she wanted to argue, or was in one of her piques. But I never gave her that satisfaction. I would simply walk away, leaving her to shout alone. It became quite an enjoyable game with me.

"Then, on one of my trips to Baltimore several years ago, I met a lady of singular qualities." Henry gazed out the window behind Philip. "She is intelligent, warm and gentle. Everything Ursula is not. This lady became my safe haven."

Caught off guard, Philip dropped the silver letter opener he had been toying with.

"Shocked?"

Clearing his throat, Philip stammered, "Well, yes--and no. It explains why I never observed any affection pass between you and Mother. I often wondered how you could endure a loveless marriage. A misery I know all too well," he added with a sigh. "Elizabeth informed me several months ago that she wants no child of mine to interfere with her social schedule and moved into the guest suite. At least Mother provided you with heirs first."

Henry chuckled again. "That was because my father exerted great pressure on her to do so. Old Jasper was the only living being who could intimidate Ursula. One glance from him usually scared the hell out of her. It was a wonder to behold. But I could not divorce her. I am a Creighton, my father kept reminding me. I must never do anything to sully the honorable family name. So, I took my solace in Baltimore."

"Does Mother know?"

"I suspect she does, but she doesn't give a damn. It leaves her free to indulge in her life's work of meddling and manipulating." Henry contemplated a moment before continuing, "Philip, I vowed I would never do this but, heaven help me, I cannot keep silent any longer." His shrewd, thoughtful eyes softened. "You cannot hide from whatever it is that is affecting your health. My advice is to face up to your problems. And promise me that you will see a doctor."

"Forgive me if I sound cynical, Pa, but how can a doctor help? Can he undo my mistakes? Or restore my trust?"

"Son, only you can undo your mistakes. As for those who have abused your trust, there are ways of making them regret it." Nodding, he gave Philip a knowing wink.

Grinning in response, Philip pondered the possibilities.

Henry glanced at his pocket watch and rose abruptly. "I didn't realize it was so late. I will have to hurry if I want to catch my train."

"I'll walk you to your carriage, Pa."

Henry regarded Philip with deep affection. "When I return, I expect to see you looking better than you do now."

"Yes, sir." Seeing Henry's frown, Philip added, "All right, I will even see a doctor."

Smiling, he patted Philip's shoulder. "Good."

Philip choked back his rising emotions. "Thank you, Pa. It is nice to know that someone understands and cares about me. I'm glad we had this discussion. By the way, where will you be in case I need to contact you?"

"In Baltimore," Henry smiled.

Philip returned his smile then his expression turned serious. "Be careful, Pa. This secession issue is heating up and, as you are undoubtedly aware, Maryland is pro-Southern in its sympathies, and the standoff down there at Fort Sumter is only exacerbating the matter. I just heard that Georgia is now the fifth state to secede from the Union. Hell,

Robert Strickland is even talking about raising a cavalry company if a war comes."

"I pray it never comes to that. Besides," Henry added with a wry smile, "I am fully aware of current events. I read the family newspaper."

Chapter 20

AFTER HENRY'S DEPARTURE, Philip returned to the mail that had accumulated during his week-long absence. Under an envelope from a hotel marked 'personal', he found a bill from a carriage maker, whose name he did not recognize. Slitting open the envelope, he nearly strangled at the statement marked 'unattended debt' for the phaeton Elizabeth had ordered.

"Damn it," he swore aloud, and tossed the statement aside. "We shall see about this."

Next, he opened an envelope from the Strand Hotel. It contained an overdue statement from the caterer for the wedding reception. "Why in the hell is the hotel sending this to me when it should have gone to Arthur Stockton?" he asked aloud, his face now purple with rage.

Swiveling his chair around, Philip gazed out the window, recalling the advice Henry had given him a few moments ago, 'As for those who have abused your trust, there are ways of making them regret it'.

"Sound advice, Pa," he muttered to himself. "However, retribution need not be swift. It must be perfect--and inflict as much damage as possible."

* * *

Barely an hour later, Tom Dayton ushered in Mr. Welles, who came in response to Philip's urgent summons.

"Thank you for coming so promptly, Mr. Welles," Philip began in his terse business voice. "I will not take much of your time. I received your statement concerning my wife's phaeton. I believed this matter had been resolved."

Mr. Welles assumed a doleful expression. "I'm sorry, sir. I may have misunderstood your wife's instructions when I gave her the bill upon delivery in November. After all these months, I decided that I had indeed erred, and felt the matter should have been directed to your attention."

Hearing that Elizabeth had known about this bill all along, Philip struggled to keep his face a mask. So, here is another lie attributed to my dear wife. "I will take care of it now," he informed Mr. Welles in a voice that sounded calm and reasonable, even to his own ears, "and we will consider the matter closed."

Mr. Welles bowed. "As you wish, sir. I apologize for this inconvenience."

He waited patiently while Philip wrote the check with a remarkably steady hand, his lips compressed until white lines appeared at the corners.

Mr. Welles could hardly have been out the door when Tom announced that the hotel caterer, Mr. Bascombe, had already arrived. A small man, with gray hair and mustache, and impeccably dressed in a dark pinstriped suit, the caterer seated himself at Philip's desk.

Philip flung the statement across the desk at him. "May I ask why this was sent to me?"

Retrieving the statement, Mr. Bascombe studied it carefully. "I sent this to Mr. Stockton in September, then in October, and again in November. The December statement was returned with this note from Mr. Stockton," he said in a precise manner, handing the statement to Philip.

Philip read the message written in Arthur's own hand, instructing Mr. Bascombe to send the invoice to Philip's office for payment. "I see," he said, realizing that there was nothing for it but to pay the damned thing if he were to maintain his own reputation in the business community.

After Mr. Bascombe left with Philip's assurance of prompt payment, Philip paced behind his desk, fuming. What the hell did Stockton do with all the money I lent him for the wedding? Women? Gambling debts? And, more to the point, does he intend to repay the loan since he has made no mention of it to me?

Damn it, I should go straight to his house right now and throttle him to within an inch of his larcenous life for causing me this embarrassment.

Throwing his cheroot into the fire, he went back to his desk to look over the rest of the mail. There he found several more statements from Elizabeth's many shopping sprees, worsening his dark mood. "By God," he muttered, smashing his fist onto his desk, "there must be an end to it. She and her father must learn that I am not their personal banker."

He wrote a brutally blunt note and had it delivered by messenger to the Stockton home.

When Philip arrived home later that day, he was still trembling with fury. He stalked down the hall toward Elizabeth's room as her door opened and she stepped out. "Philip, is that you?"

"Were you expecting someone else? Julian perhaps?" he snapped.

She blanched. "Don't be ridiculous. I just wanted to remind you that I am having dinner at Papa's this evening."

"That being the case, perhaps I should warn you that he may mention the note I sent him this afternoon wherein I called him a lying, thieving bastard."

Her mouth flew open, but he raised his hand to silence her. "Don't bother protesting. I am fully aware of his duplicitous action of having the catering bill for the wedding sent to me. Past due, of course. And for which expense I advanced him a considerable sum." He waved the other bills under her nose. "You and I will also have a little chat about these and a few other matters. Won't you join me?" He indicated that she accompany him to his bedroom.

She walked ahead of him, stood in the middle of his room, her hands on her hips, waiting.

"Now," he flung them at her one at a time, "here is the one from Worth's for all those gowns you bought last month, and the ones for jewelry, and Mr. Baldwin's long overdue bill for the cook's and maids' uniforms, and Ames' livery. Last and certainly not the least of which is the considerable sum for your phaeton.

"Mr. Welles informed me this morning that he gave you a statement in November when he delivered the phaeton. I can see by your surprised expression that you did not intend for me to find this out, did you? Having been misled by your expert acting, I am sure Mr. Welles believed payment would be forthcoming. When he received none, he sent the bill to the poor dumb husband to see if that would evoke a response."

"You said you could afford it," she defended herself.

"That is not the issue," he shouted back. "Your lies are the issues. And I will not address your complete disregard for the social proprieties that are expected of you as my wife." Without waiting for her reaction, he continued, "As for the money I loaned your father for that farcical wedding, I intend to see that he repays every damned cent."

"Are you expecting payment from me too? I have no money of my own, but I think I know what you want." Opening her kimono with a flourish, she let it drop to the floor.

He circled her, assessing her as one assesses prime horseflesh. "Not good enough."

"There was a time," she began seductively.

"That was long ago," he said with a smirk. "It is amazing how stupid a man can be when he is blinded by what he believes is love. Now that I am unencumbered by that emotion, all I see is a pretty young woman who has grown fat from over-indulgence. I also see a woman who will be hard pressed to incur any more debts.

"Yes, my dear," he said at her surprised expression, "I have instructed all the establishments where I do business not to extend credit to any member of my family or to my in-laws. The household items and food will be purchased by the cook and the housekeeper and I will check those bills weekly."

"You would dare do such a thing?" she screamed.

"You speak to me of being daring? You and your father are two of the most daring criminals I have ever met. But rest assured that I have only begun to curb your wanton ways."

He leaned against his armoire, a dark smile creasing his face. "I cannot wait to see how amorous Julian will be once he learns that your source of revenue has been cut off. And you can tell Julian for me that he will never get his greedy hands on one more cent of the Creighton money. Don't look so shocked, my dear. Do you really believe that I did not know where you went, or with whom, when you disappeared for days at a time? Your error was in mistaking my silence for weakness."

He started to turn away then, remembering something else, he added, "By the way, you had better pray that Mother never learns of your little scheme to defraud me or there will be worse hell to pay. Retaliation by Ursula Creighton could be far more devastating than you--or anyone--could ever envision. And put your kimono back on." He waved his arm in dismissal. "You have long since lost your appeal."

Scooping the kimono from the floor, she slung it around her shoulders. "How dare you insult me like this."

"Madam, for the money I have invested in you, I will insult you any way I please."

Shouldering his way past her, he poured a drink from the decanter and tossed it off in one gulp, smiling at the sound of the door slamming as punctuation to her forced retreat.

Chapter 21

PHILIP SAT IN his closed carriage, staring at the envelope that arrived in this morning's mail just as he was leaving for his daily inspection tour of the construction site. He knew it contained the results of the physical examination by his doctor that he'd agreed to in deference to his father's wishes, and to satisfy his own curiosity. With trembling fingers, Philip tore into the envelope and read confirmation of the doctor's findings--a malaise of unknown origin.

He crumpled the paper and muttered aloud, "I damned well know its origin--Elizabeth and her antics." But before she ruins my health as well as my life, he decided, I must take hold of my own destiny. I would love to throw the bitch out, divorce her, anything to get her out of my life. That, however, would create a far worse firestorm than the war that now seems so imminent. But, he thought with a twisted smile, perhaps therein is my solution. I will have to wait and see.

Arriving at the hilltop construction, Philip alighted from his carriage into the blustery late February wind. Due to the severe weather, the job foreman, Mr. Ramsey, was forced to halt all work. Philip walked around the deserted site, inspecting the work that had been completed so far. Inside Mr. Ramsey's shed, they discussed what should be done next, and what materials had been ordered.

Mr. Ramsey gazed with pride through the work shed window at the partially-constructed mansion. "It's going to be a beauty, Mr. Creighton. There'll be none like it for miles around."

"Yes," Philip replied, suddenly uninterested in the project, "it is coming along nicely."

While studying the sketch of the finished house, a strange light filled his eyes. "Of course, it's perfect," he whispered, as though to himself. "Why didn't I think of it before?"

At the unusual expression on Philip's face, Mr. Ramsey turned toward him, concerned. "Are you all right, sir? You look kinda strange."

"Yes, yes, I'm fine, Mr. Ramsey. Never better," he said, clapping the foreman on the shoulder, and left the shed, smiling.

The wind swirled around the crest of the hilltop as Philip's matched mares, snorting frosty plumes, pulled his carriage across the frozen ground. He'd waited weeks until the weather had turned bitter cold before insisting that Elizabeth accompany him to the construction site.

"I don't see why you are dragging me up here in this awful weather," she grumbled, and snuggled down further under the fur lap robe.

"Stop whining," Philip said. "I want to show you something."

"It had better be good. I am frozen to the bone." Her eyes and nose were the only facial features visible between her fur hat and the lap robe.

"Believe me, it will be," he said with a smirk.

When the carriage stopped in front of the partially completed house, they alighted. Philip said to his driver, "All right, Martin, you may leave to warm yourself. Come back for us later."

"Thank you, sir," Martin said with obvious gratitude, and drove away.

"Where are the workmen?" Elizabeth asked, casting a wary eye around the abandoned site, and pulled her sable coat up around her chin.

"I couldn't expect them to work under these conditions so I told them to lay down their tools and go home. I have shut down the entire project." Ignoring Elizabeth's sputtering, he called to Mr. Ramsey inside the shed, "Before you leave, I would like the house plans."

"Certainly, sir," Mr. Ramsey called back. "I'll get them before I lock everything up."

Appearing a moment later, he handed the rolled-up plans to Philip.

"Thank you, Mr. Ramsey. By the way, please submit the figures on how much I owe your men and all the other workmen you hired to do the inside specialty work. Also, get the figures on the supplies ordered so far, like the marble, stained glass and so forth, cancel the orders and send me an itemized list. I will see that everyone gets paid. With a little extra for you and your men," Philip added.

"I'll do that. Thank you, sir. Good-bye." Mr. Ramsey tipped his hat to Elizabeth and left.

Philip turned back to her. "Come, I will take you on a tour. As you can see, the second story and attic are now enclosed." He led her inside the first floor, describing where the Italian marble floor would be laid, the red oak-paneled library, and what was to be done next.

Elizabeth inspected every nook and cranny. "They have not accomplished much since the weather turned nasty."

"There is something else I want you to see." He led her through the house to the double-door frame at the back and out onto the outline of the verandah, with its sweeping view of the valley below. The wind that swirled down toward the valley took their breath away.

"What is it?" she asked through chattering teeth.

"There," he pointed down to Creighton's Crossroads where lights twinkled in the rapidly descending dusk. "Didn't you tell me that you planned to look down on the town from here?" Philip turned toward her with narrowed eyes. "You love looking down on people, don't you?"

She gave him a puzzled look. "You are acting so strangely today."

"Am I?" With a malicious grin, he held up the house plans. "You see these? They are the plans for your beautiful mansion." Before her horrified gaze, he ripped them in two with a flourish then tore them into quarters. Before she could react, he tossed the shreds into the fire barrel the workmen used to burn debris, and to warm their hands. He struck a Lucifer and threw it into the barrel. The paper and wood scraps caught and flared in an instant, fanned by the wind.

"God, that felt good," he said, brushing his gloved hands together.

"Have you lost your mind, you fool?" she screamed, and ran to retrieve the plans from the flaming barrel.

He grabbed her wrists. "Let the damned things burn. I once told you that I always planned to build a house here for my future wife and family. Well, I have no wife and I will sure as hell never have a family with you."

Elizabeth freed herself from his grip and jammed her hands inside her sable muff.

"I have been planning this for quite some time," he said in a light tone of voice that still had an edge to it. "I just wanted to make sure the house was far enough along so that losing it would be as painful as possible for you." He glared down at her. "It's not a pretty feeling being strung along, is it?

"You see, several months ago, I began fitting the pieces of the puzzle together. My mother and her meddling. You and your avaricious father, and your part in the grand scheme of things. So, since November, I have kept a mental account of each new lie and outrageous act and deprived you, little by little. My first action, you will recall, was cutting off your accounts.

"But I also knew that whatever final retribution I chose to visit upon you must be perfect." Casting a pleased look at the flames dancing and leaping from the barrel, he asked with a chilling smile, "Don't you think this is perfect?"

"What I think is that you have lost your mind. I will not let you stop construction on my house," she said, and rushed past him toward the trash barrel. "I won't let you burn these plans."

He chuckled, hard and mirthless. "You won't *let* me? Elizabeth, you are amazing. Did you really believe that, given your wanton behavior, I would ever let you live in this house?" With a taunting smile, he pressed his right foot against the mid-section of the barrel.

Seeing what he intended, she cried, "You wouldn't! Dear God, you have taken leave of your senses."

Without a word, Philip gave the barrel a sharp thrust with his foot, tipping it onto its side toward the framed doorway and scattering the flaming contents across the ground floor of the house.

"Oh my God!" she shrieked. Hiking up her skirts, she stomped furiously at the tongues of flame erupting around her. The fire began spreading rapidly across the inside rooms and climbed up the framework toward the second story. "Help me, damn you. I won't let you burn my house. It's mine!" She continued her struggle against the flames.

"Nothing is yours that I don't give you," he said through clenched teeth. "You are laboring under the delusion that everyone owes you something. Now," he waved his hand at the burning structure, "it affords me a great deal of pleasure to destroy the last of what matters most to you.

But," he turned a dark malicious grin on her, "the real fun will begin when you try explaining all this to the town you so graciously planned to look down upon."

She glared at him. "You can't do this to me. What will people say?"

"I don't give a damn any more what people say. You notice that I do not apologize for my vulgar language," he said with a mock bow. "You see, I owe you no apologies--for anything.

"Although, I must compliment you on your performances in New York and Berkeley Springs," he said in the deceptively light tone he'd used earlier. "You were very good. You even had me convinced. You really should go on the stage. Or into the business. I'm sorry, I forgot. You are already in the business of prostitution, aren't you?"

"How dare you," she muttered, and started toward him.

Unfazed by her menacing expression, he continued, "In case you haven't already gotten the message, I want nothing more to do with you. You will continue to go your way and I will do as I damn well please. Although I much prefer that you leave my house. Whatever you do, it is immaterial to me. I, on the other hand, am considering a contingent plan, depending on the outcome of certain outside events"

As he spoke, the fire continued to crackle and spread closer to Elizabeth. He glanced behind her and called out, "Look out, your dress is on fire."

Seeing that the hem of her dress was smoldering, Elizabeth screamed as she threw herself to the frozen ground where the two of them beat furiously at her skirts. After making sure that the sparks were extinguished, Philip yanked her none too gently to her feet.

"How are you going to explain all this to Papa?" he asked with a smirk.

"Go to hell," she snapped, breathless from exertion, and continued brushing her skirt.

"Why, Mrs. Creighton, your unladylike language shocks me. If you aren't careful, I may become disillusioned where your character is concerned."

"You are despicable." Hearing the timbers falling in on one another, she whirled around with a gasp and stared at the destruction of her dream home.

Backing away from the rising heat, Philip watched with hard-eyed satisfaction.

She swung around to face him, her eyes narrowed into slits. "Damn you. Damn you for doing this to me. I have always hated you, but never more than at this very moment."

Philip gripped her upper arms until she winced. "Madam," he said in a chilling voice easily heard above the mounting inferno, "this is just the beginning."

They stood outlined against the spectacular inferno that lit up the hilltop and could be seen for miles, glaring at one another at close range until Philip shoved her away with a disgusted snort. At the sound of an approaching carriage, they quickly composed themselves before Ames jumped down from the driver's box of Elizabeth's phaeton and ran toward them.

"Mr. Creighton," Ames shouted, "I saw the flames and came as quickly as I could."

"There is no need for concern," Philip answered in a calm voice. "We were never in any danger."

"I have already notified the fire brigade, sir," Ames said, as he eyed Elizabeth's disheveled appearance.

"Thank you, Ames. I will keep an eye on things until Martin comes back for me. However, I would appreciate it if you would drive Mrs.

Creighton home." Philip thrust Elizabeth toward her chauffeur. "She seems a trifle distraught."

"Very well," Ames said, clearly puzzled.

Turning his back on the damning glare Elizabeth fixed on him, Philip stood with his hands clasped behind his back and watched as his grand house collapsed into charred ruins. In the distance, he could hear the bells of the fire brigade as it rapidly approached.

Chapter 22

AFTER BATHING AND washing the smell of acrid smoke from her hair, Elizabeth stood before her bedroom window wrapped in a red velvet robe, oblivious to the sleet hissing against the glass. She stared into the dark, recalling the events of that afternoon, the horror of seeing Philip reduce her dreams to ashes. Damn him. And damn Julian for being wrong about Philip. He is, as she feared, a force to be reckoned with.

Realizing the full scope of her dilemma for the first time, she scolded herself for being a damned fool. You have gone too far, too fast. And now your world is falling down around you.

The sound of her father's excited voice in the lower hall brought her back to the moment. "Elizabeth! Elizabeth, where are you?"

She gripped the fold of the drapes. My God, how could he have found out so soon? But, she recalled with dread, given the size of that blaze, everyone in town must have seen it.

A moment later, Arthur stood in the upstairs hall, puffing and panting from his hasty climb up the stairs. "Where in the hell are you?" he called again, looking around in the semi-darkness.

She stood in the doorway to her room, a shadowy figure clutching her robe around her, her hair still damp. "Hello, Papa," she said in a strained voice.

"Don't hello me, miss," he shouted, his face crimson with rage.

Arthur shouldered his way past her into the bedroom and stalked about, mopping the perspiration from his face, despite the frigid temperatures. "I overheard Philip's foreman Ramsey telling everyone in the hotel bar that Philip stopped construction on the mansion over a week ago, without so much as a how-do-you-do. Said he couldn't figure why he did it. And now, this mysterious fire." He fixed a suspicious eye on her. "What do you know about this?"

"About what?" she asked, and mentally damned Ramsey for blabbing their business abroad.

"Don't play innocent with me. You know damned well what I'm talking about. What would make Philip do such a thing?" he asked, squinting into her terrified eyes. "Could it have been in retaliation for some of your shenanigans? I warned you--"

He stopped his ranting long enough to look around the room at her personal belongings strewn about. "Isn't this the guest room? What are you doing in here?" he demanded, his voice rising to fever pitch. "Why aren't you in the master suite?"

"Philip and I are sleeping separately now."

"Sleeping separately? After only seven months? Why would...?" Understanding dawned in his eyes. "You damned fool! Was sleeping separately his idea--or yours?"

Elizabeth turned away from his accusing eyes.

Arthur slammed his fist against the back of a chair. "What on earth possessed you? Answer me, damn you, before I take a buggy whip to you."

"Calm down, Papa. It's not as bad as all that. We just came to an agreement, that's all."

He shook a finger under her nose. "If you tell me that you are involved with someone else and Philip found out about it, I *will* take a buggy whip to you. I have told you time and again that you must maintain control. You cannot do that from the guest suite. Damn it all, you may have ruined everything."

Still puffing from exertion, Arthur paused to pass a handkerchief over his face again. "After hearing Ramsey's story," he resumed in a ragged voice, "I decided to stop by the Creighton house to see if they had heard about the fire. Well, let me tell you, there are no secrets in this damned town. The old lady was in high rare form, ranting on and on about Philip losing his mind and letting the house burn like that, and what would people think."

Elizabeth turned toward him with a start, remembering Philip's prediction about dire consequences if Ursula ever found out that she and Arthur had duped her. "Ursula knows?"

"Yes, and my God, I have never seen her in such a state. She was castigating Philip for embarrassing her before the town. 'Everyone will talk,' she kept wailing."

"What about Mr. Creighton?" she asked. "He rarely offers an opinion, but he is the one who really frightens me. I never know what he's thinking."

"Henry wasn't saying much tonight either. Just stared straight ahead and let the old woman vent her anger. And he had the strangest smile on his face, like he knew something the rest of us didn't." Arthur shook his head in wonder. "I never could fathom the man."

He resumed his pacing, and pounded a fist into the palm of his other hand. "Do you have any idea what Philip might do next?"

Offering no response, Elizabeth stared out her window at the wind-driven sleet.

"Oh, my God," Arthur groaned. "We were so close to having it all and now you--you have done something stupid. Didn't I warn you to be discreet? Well," he said, recovering himself, "you will just have to rectify the situation."

"How do you propose I do that?"

"Do whatever it takes, damn it, but get back into Philip's good graces. Do you hear me? I strongly suggest that you begin by moving back into the master suite. We cannot let everything we have worked and planned for slip through our fingers because of your thoughtlessness."

Shaking his head, Arthur squinted at her. "Something about you has given me many sleepless nights." He waited until she turned to face him with a look that was at once curious but uncaring. "I have always suspected that my own dear daughter may have fewer scruples than

I and that someday you would bring us to this. And now you have confirmed those fears."

He stomped around the room, cursing and muttering, stopping long enough to shake his fist at her. "We planned so carefully for this and now--oh, my God!" he cried, and threw up his hands in frustration.

Clenching her fists inside the folds of her robe, Elizabeth said with great control to hide her own trembling, "Don't forget, Papa, I am not the only one who has done something to incur Philip's wrath. You should never have had the hotel caterer send Philip the bill for the wedding. That is what started all of this. We will just have to think of something else to do. And," she added with genuine fear, "pray that Ursula Creighton never learns the truth."

After the furor over the fire subsided, time had no meaning or place in Philip's life. Nor was he aware of the passing of time. Each day seemed like the last, neither rushed, nor long and drawn out. He simply filled his mind with business affairs, and planned extended trips away from Crossroads.

Gradually though, he slipped into the routine of more social contact with his long-time friends whom he felt he had neglected during his brief, disastrous marriage. Together, he and Denton Cobb, his closest friend, gathered with Robert Strickland and Leland Myles to resume their weekly poker games.

At other times, Philip and his father met for dinner at a local hotel, or in Harrisburg, or any place that afforded them privacy. During one of their dinners, Philip at last confided to Henry his reasons for burning down the house.

Henry voiced his approval and ordered a bottle of champagne. "I suspected that may have been the case. I told you," he added with a wink, "that there are ways to make people sorry."

At the time, Philip couldn't help wondering what Henry had in store for Ursula.

Philip was unsuccessful, however, in removing Elizabeth from his home but he had no problem avoiding her. She continued to absent herself from Crossroads for days at a time, yet he remained indifferent as to where she went or what she was doing. As far as he was concerned, Julian was more than welcome to that faithless baggage.

During all of February and March, he kept a vigilant eye on the sectional differences that threatened to tear the country apart. The Confederate constitution had already been adopted and Jefferson Davis elected president of the seceded states. President Lincoln had been inaugurated on March 4, 1861. His speech reminded everyone that he had the oath registered in heaven to preserve the Union and he meant to do just that. And now there was the stand-off at Fort Sumter.

Everything seemed to be moving ahead toward armed conflict as though it were preordained. Nothing could stop it.

Philip worried over these disquieting events, as the pressure toward war mounted with each passing day. He watched, he waited, and he bided his time.

Chapter 23

IN ANSWER TO a frantic summons from the newspaper editor, Philip left his office at the bank and hurried up the plank sidewalk toward the newspaper building. Along the way, he noticed that excited crowds were gathered in small groups and pointed with animation toward the newspaper office.

Curious and alarmed by the excitement, he entered the newspaper office where all was in chaos. The editor, Harry Slade, was issuing frantic orders to the typesetters. "I thought you might want to see this," Slade barked to Philip above the noise in the printing room. He thrust a copy of a special afternoon edition of the *Creighton's Crossroads Herald* into Philip's hands.

Philip glanced at the bold headline then read with dismay the lead article recounting the lengthy standoff at Fort Sumter in Charleston harbor, and the subsequent bombardment of the federal installation by Confederate sympathizers the day before, April 12. Another headline announced that President Lincoln had issued a call to arms.

He fell into Mr. Slade's chair. "Well, here it is, Harry," he shouted in a voice that could barely be heard above the clatter of the printing press. "During all those weeks of the stand-off at the fort, I hoped cooler heads would prevail."

"Yeh, well, apparently, the South Carolina hot-spurs didn't see it that way," Slade remarked with a cigar clenched between stained teeth.

"Don't they realize what they're asking, by forcing armed conflict? This is madness."

As Philip pondered the ramifications of this inflammatory incident, Elizabeth appeared at the door, sobbing incoherently. "There you are, Philip. Come quickly, I need you."

"What is it?" he asked with an impatient frown. "Can't you see that I'm busy? The war has started and..." Seeing genuine terror in her eyes, he knew instinctively that she would never have come to him for anything if it were not a true emergency.

"It's Papa," she cried.

He jumped up from the chair and pulled her outside Slade's office. "Get hold of yourself, girl. What happened to your father?"

"He may be dead," she managed to say between sobs.

Grabbing her by the hand, he led her outside to the waiting phaeton. Once they were seated inside, he asked her to tell him as calmly as she could exactly what happened.

"I'm not really sure. He--he and another man were in the library, arguing." She caught her breath in ragged gasps. "I don't know who the man was. After he left, I--I went into the library. Papa was highly agitated. Told me not to worry. To pour him a brandy. But before--before he could take a drink, he had this great seizure and made a strange gurgling sound. Nothing I did revived him." She buried her face in her trembling hands and sobbed harder.

"Did someone send for a doctor?"

"Mother sent the maid for Dr. Haskell." Leaning against the side of the phaeton completely spent, she stared into space.

Feeling he should console her, Philip started to put his arm around her but the instinct was no longer there. Instead, he wondered about the argument Elizabeth had mentioned. In a town this size, it shouldn't be difficult to learn who had argued with Arthur.

When Philip and Elizabeth arrived at the Stockton home, Dr. Haskell was in the foyer, consoling Mary. The maid stood in the back of the hall, sniffling and drying her eyes.

Philip took Dr. Haskell aside. "Can you tell yet what happened?"

"From my initial examination, it appears he died of a massive heart attack."

Elizabeth broke into fresh sobs and turned to Philip for comfort. For the sake of appearances, he was forced to put his arms around her. At one time, his arms had ached to hold her but now he found the act unnatural, and somewhat disgusting.

The next three days were a blur for Philip. Feeling compelled to assist the bewildered Mary Stockton, he saw to the funeral arrangements, and the many other details that arose.

The reading of Arthur Stockton's will was a simple affair. He had nothing to leave his wife but the house and a mountain of debts. At Mary's insistence, Philip agreed to look into Arthur's financial affairs. As he leafed through the pile of unpaid bills and the bank records, he wondered how Arthur could have been so financially irresponsible and not been caught long before this.

Was Arthur really that stupid, or had he simply taken advantage of the blindness and trust of the entire town?

A week after Arthur's funeral, Tom Dayton entered Philip's office and informed him that there were three gentlemen waiting to see him. "They said their business was urgent."

"Yes, everyone's business is urgent," Philip muttered. "Show in the first one to arrive."

"They all arrived together, sir."

"Together?" Philip peered through the door to the outer office. "Who is out there?"

"Mr. Winston from the Strand Hotel, Mr. Myles from the mercantile store and," Tom consulted his notes, "a Mr. Wexford. They seem quite agitated."

"Well, if they arrived together, I have no choice but to see them together."

Philip stood as the three men entered his office. He exchanged handshakes before inviting them to be seated. Mr. Winston sat in the chair before Philip's desk and crossed his legs. He was a trim man, a meticulous dresser with an eye for detail. As manager of the town's most elegant hotel, he was always anxious to please his clientele but never effusive in his demeanor.

Mr. Myles, whom Philip had known since childhood, owned the largest mercantile store in Crossroads. He sat on the leather sofa beside an unfamiliar gentleman, apparently the Mr. Wexford Tom had mentioned.

"What may I do for you gentlemen?" Philip asked.

After some foot shuffling and throat clearing, Mr. Winston reached into his coat pocket. "I apologize for this intrusion during this difficult time for your family, Mr. Creighton, but we were given to understand that you were handling Mr. Stockton's affairs."

"That's true. Did you have dealings with him?" Philip felt a sudden tightening in his gut.

"I hesitate bringing this up but, being a businessman, you can appreciate my position."

"Certainly." Keeping his face as bland as possible, Philip seethed, knowing these men were about to bombard him with even more past-due debts of his late father-in-law. Like his dear daughter, he thought, Arthur fancied that the world owed him a living.

Philip turned to William Myles, a rotund man, and every inch the smiling, hand-shaking businessman. Philip knew that he was also very shrewd.

Mr. Myles tugged at his cravat before beginning, "As you can see, Philip, this amount is considerable. For some reason, Mr. Stockton was hesitant to pay anything toward the balance. I pressed him as much as I dared, his being a gentleman and all. When I last spoke with him, he advised me that he had made arrangements with you to take care of the entire matter."

Philip glanced at Mr. Myles' bill totaling over two thousand dollars. "Is this for items purchased by Mr. Stockton's family?" he asked in a surprisingly even voice.

"That is correct. Some of the purchases were made by your lovely wife just prior to your marriage."

Damn you, Arthur, Philip swore silently, for reaching into my checkbook from the grave.

He swiveled his chair toward the hotel manager. "How much is your bill?"

Mr. Winston hesitated before answering, "You must understand, Mr. Creighton, the owners of the hotel have been pressing me on this. Naturally, I am obliged to act."

"How much?"

"Slightly more than three thousand dollars."

"What in the world could he have done to run up a bill in that amount?" he asked, and wondered if Arthur had been keeping a mistress.

"Mr. Stockton advised me that his business required a great deal of entertaining. Most of the charges are from the dining room and bar."

Without further comment, Philip turned his attention to the silent but watchful Mr. Wexford. Unlike the other two conservatively dressed gentlemen, his appearance spoke of easy money acquired by means better left unsaid. He wore a flashy plaid suit with a large gold watch fob that dangled from a massive chain draped across his equally massive stomach. The florid red cheeks alerted Philip that the man liked his drinks.

"So, Mr. Wexford, what can I do for you?" Philip asked with an edge in his voice.

Exhibiting none of the reticence displayed by Mr. Myles or Mr. Winston, he withdrew a paper from the inside pocket of his coat and placed it on top of the hotel bill.

"May I ask what this is for, sir?" Philip asked after glancing at it.

"A gambling debt Arthur incurred several years ago. I had backed him in several ventures over the years. It pains me to say it, but he had accumulated considerable losses. On this particular date," Mr. Wexford tapped his finger on the agreement, "he gave me a ten thousand dollar mortgage on his home, payable upon demand.

"This note has always been a source of contention between us. We even argued about it the day he died. Under the circumstances, I feel like a cad, but," he hunched his shoulders, "you can understand my position, sir. This is strictly business."

Leaning back in his chair, Philip studied the cigar-chewing businessman. *So, that answers the question about who argued with Arthur the day he died.*

He swiveled his chair away from them and stared into the fireplace. *What choice do I have but to satisfy these debts, more to save my own name than Arthur's? How ironic that I seem to have been his only asset.* Heaving a reluctant sigh, Philip realized he had no choice but to write each of these men a draft.

Turning to face them, he said, "Gentlemen, I appreciate your candor and your patience. If you will step into the anteroom, I will write each of you a bank draft. I pray that is agreeable."

"Most agreeable. Thank you, sir." Mr. Wexford smiled as he followed the others outside.

Philip stirred himself from his bitter thoughts and reached for his pen. He wrote the drafts through a thin red haze of anger that had fallen before his eyes halfway through the interview. When he finished writing the three drafts, he rang for Tom and instructed him to give the sealed envelopes to each of the gentlemen.

"Yes, sir." Tom left Philip's office, eyeing the sealed envelopes surreptitiously.

Philip poured a drink to steady his nerves, but his fury at being used again by Arthur could not be contained. He swept his hand across the top of his desk, sending the overdue statements, documents and a glass paper weight flying.

"Damn your black soul!" he shouted, as the bills fluttered to the floor. "It had to come to this sooner or later, didn't it? You expected me to pay your way through life and your daughter was the ticket. Well, sir, we shall see about that."

Storming from his office, he stalked blindly onto the sidewalk in front of the bank where he collided with his friend, Robert Strickland. As tall as Philip, with light brown hair and brown eyes, Robert flashed an easy smile. "Whoa, there, Philip. What's your hurry?"

"Sorry, Robert, my mind was elsewhere." Taking a deep breath to calm himself, Philip asked, "How is the recruiting going for the cavalry company?"

"Quite well. Since Fort Sumter, feelings are running high. That's the time to get recruits." Robert tapped Philip's shoulder. "I still need officers. Have you given any thought to joining the cavalry unit? You would start with a major's commission."

"As a matter of fact," Philip said, "you are just the fellow I want to see. I have been giving serious thought to that very thing the past few months. However, there are some urgent matters that I must take care of before I make a final decision. I will see you in the morning."

"Good," Robert smiled. "I will be waiting for you at the enlistment office next to the milliner's shop."

Shaking Robert's hand, Philip realized that the world was going mad just now, shrinking his own problems into relative insignificance.

He crossed the street to the Fairview Hotel bar, avoiding the Strand Hotel where he might encounter Mr. Winston. In the less sumptuous Fairview, he ordered a drink to help him face the ordeal, not unlike this war, that had been brewing far too long.

Chapter 24

IN THE APRIL twilight, the gloomy house was silent. Going straight to his room, Philip tore off his clothes and threw them into the nearest chair instead of hanging them neatly, as was his habit. Slipping on his dressing robe, he slumped into a fireside chair with a drink.

He stared out the window at the hilltop, now shrouded in darkness, where the charred remains of his unfinished mansion lay and recalled with grim satisfaction that delicious moment of retribution when he reduced Elizabeth's dreams to ashes. That had been his most satisfying act since the sorry day he first met her.

A soft knock on the door broke into his thoughts, jolting him back to the moment. "Dinner is served, sir," Sally called through the door. "Mrs. Creighton has already gone down to the dining room."

A dark, humorless smile creased Philip's face. At last, the moment has arrived. "Thank you, Sally," he said aloud. "I will be down directly."

Finishing the last of the bourbon, he placed the glass on the lamp table, stood up, and made his way unsteadily downstairs to the dining room. He slid the doors open with a dramatic flourish and stood with his arms outstretched on the doorjambs for support. "Good evening, my dear. Are we alone?"

Elizabeth looked up with a start. "Yes, and thank goodness we are. How dare you appear at the table in that shocking attire?"

"Is it my dress that offends you, or that I am well into my cups? Oh well," he shrugged, "who the hell cares?"

"You are drunk," she huffed.

"But not drunk enough." He strode into the dining room and, clutching the back of his chair for support, he fixed a hard eye on her. "Do you know why I am drunk? Because of your dear departed father who ran through Crossroads yelling 'Charge, and send the bills to my stupid son-in-law.' Well, his stupid son-in-law had his stupid eyes opened this morning."

Throwing down her napkin, Elizabeth started to rise. "I will not sit here and listen to you defame my father's memory."

"Oh, yes, you will listen." The tone of his voice intimidated her back into her seat. "Today, in order to save your poor mother from being dispossessed and thrown into the street, I wrote three checks totaling fifteen thousand dollars." At her startled reaction, he smirked. "I thought those figures would get your attention."

Her eyes became defensive, wary. "I have no idea what you are babbling about."

"It seems that your dear departed father had advised his many, and I might add desperate, creditors that I would take care of his debts. Given the circumstances, what else could I do but pay them? After all, my own reputation was at stake."

He circled the table, running his index finger over the damask tablecloth. "Which brings me to the matter at hand. I have long since grown tired of being your personal ticket for a soft, easy life." He stopped at the head of the table and slammed his fist on it so forcibly that the dishes and candles danced. "Well, by God, no more. I came to inform you that I am leaving you."

"You can't walk out on me."

"Oh, no? Just watch me." He sat, leaned back in his chair and sipped his wine. Malice danced in his eyes. "I have been planning this moment since you exhibited your true colors by denying me my conjugal rights. I chose to remain silent until it suited my purposes to exact final retribution upon you, an even better one than burning down your dream house."

Rising again, he strolled around the table toward her. "Your great mistake, my dear wife, was in believing that I would be hesitant to dishonor the family name or worse yet, that I was unwilling to act. I first put my plan into motion, you will recall, when I learned that you had ordered a phaeton and hired a driver without my knowledge.

"In light of that, and your other spending frenzies, I would say that canceling your accounts was more than justified. Had you asked, I would have purchased a phaeton for you. Perhaps one even more lavish than the one you have. But I will not have things taken from me by stealth as though they were owed."

He loomed over her, glaring. "You have no conception how much you embarrassed not only me, but yourself before the town. You failed your social obligations by not returning calls from the other ladies. You also chose not to present yourself at Mother's monthly socials. You held fetes and parties for the few friends you have left--all during my out-of-town business trips." He paused, considering. "Hell, there are too many other transgressions to enumerate here."

"I can do as I please," she sniffed with disdain.

"That is where you are misinformed. The money and social position you sought with the fervor of a fanatic does not give you leave to do as you damn well please." He regarded her for a moment, his head tilted to one side. "I am curious about something. Did you really believe that I would sit back and let you run rough shod over me or use my money for your selfish pleasures? Or allow you and your father to pick my pockets without retaliating?"

"I will never divorce you, if that is what you are waiting to hear." Elizabeth rose and walked around the table to face him squarely. "I will not go through life as a marked woman. No decent man would have anything to do with me."

"You are right about no decent man, but there is always Julian."

"How dare you!" Elizabeth threw her fists at him and pounded his chest until he grasped her wrists and held her fast. "Let me go," she screamed. "You are hurting me."

He released her with a shove. "As my final liberating act, I have made a momentous decision. I am meeting Robert Strickland in the morning to do what many will perceive as my patriotic duty." Seeing her incredulous look, he nodded. "Yes, in response to President Lincoln's call, I am joining the Union army to help quell this rebellion. But look on the bright side, Mrs. Creighton. There is always the chance that I will be killed on the field of honor, which would make you a widow."

He watched as the delightful possibilities of that eventuality flickered in her eyes. Damning her silently, he turned and started toward the door.

"Would you have stayed if there had been a child?" she asked, rubbing her throbbing wrists.

He stopped. Keeping his back to her, he said, "If you are trying to seduce me, madam, don't waste your time. The thought of touching you now disgusts me."

Without another word, he stalked out of the dining room and up the stairs.

Philip locked his bedroom door and fell into the fireside chair, calling himself every kind of fool for not seeing the early danger signals. For blinding himself to Elizabeth's true nature. For allowing the pain of losing Samantha to cloud his reason.

He tossed off glass after glass from a fresh bottle of bourbon but found that he was suddenly, strangely sober.

Next morning, following a visit to Denton Cobb's law office to amend his will and make arrangements for his diverse business ventures, Philip presented himself at the enlistment office. Robert Strickland beamed with pride as the latest addition to the Strickland Pennsylvania Volunteers, Cavalry, USA, signed the enlistment papers.

Robert clapped Philip on the back. "You won't regret this, old friend. With all these good Pennsylvania men, we should whip those rebels and send them packing in no time. It will be a great adventure," he said with a wink. "You'll see."

Chapter 25

"WELL, COLONEL STRICKLAND, don't I present a pretty picture?" Philip asked, standing in the tent opening, his uniform and boots mud-splattered. "Where, I ask you, is the glory in war?"

Robert looked up from the paper work on his field desk. He had grown thin since leaving Crossroads over two years ago. A few gray hairs shone among the brown ones sorely in need of a haircut. The rigors of command had added a few wrinkles around Robert's eyes.

He assessed Philip's disheveled appearance with an indulgent smile. "I assume you are going to change before attending Miss Catlett's soiree this evening?"

Philip heaved an exasperated sigh. "I am so damned tired of all these parties. I'm ready for some action. I didn't join the army to grow fat on Washington party food and gossip."

"I feel the same way," Robert nodded. "On the other hand, it does allow Rachel and my boys to visit me once in a while. Without those visits, I would have gone mad by now."

Philip suppressed a twinge of envy at Robert's happy marriage. "Oh well," he shrugged, "at least these parties give us something else to do besides playing nurse maid to local officials or guarding supply trains. Even the troops are grumbling about inactivity."

"I know, but the President wants the city protected from possible rebel invasion."

For the last two years, the Strickland Volunteers have been encamped on Ridge Road adjacent to Fort Baker, one of the many defensive forts surrounding Washington City to guard against invasion. More than forty thousand troops occupying the make-shift forts endure boredom and endless training. To compound their misery, the hastily assembled War Department was mired in the complete mismanagement of troops and materiel.

To help dispel the everlasting boredom, the men sought entertainment wherever they could, usually in Foggy Bottom, an area of Washington notorious for its bawdy houses, gambling and murders. Harvey's Oyster Bar was also a favorite haunt of the troops. Daily, they'd stand in long lines with their buckets, waiting for an order of Harvey's famous oysters.

And then there were the endless parties which the matrons of Washington society felt duty-bound to provide for 'the boys in uniform'. On this particular evening, the officers of the Strickland Volunteers were invited to the home of Congressman Catlett and his sister, Miss Millicent, Washington's premier hostess.

"I am on my way to change my uniform now," Philip told Robert. "Are you about ready?"

Robert shook his head. "Sorry, Philip, I can't get away. This damned paperwork is never-ending. With the discipline problems, and so many on sick call, not to mention the trouble we've been having getting proper rations, I will be here all evening." He dipped his pen in the ink well. "Please convey my regrets to Miss Catlett."

"Very well. But don't work too hard," Philip called, as he headed toward the tent he shared with Captain John Wesley Madison, who joined the Strickland Volunteers during their months of training in Harrisburg.

An hour later, Philip, Captain Madison, and the new arrival, Lieutenant David Southall, made their way on horseback down Eastern

Branch Road toward Bennings Bridge. At the intersection with the Bladensburg Turnpike, they rode through the crowded Washington streets toward the Catlett home just off Lafayette Square.

On this balmy autumn evening, the streets teemed with political favor-seekers, speculators, and camp followers, not to mention the wives and families visiting the troops stationed here. Rooms in local hotels and boarding houses were always at a premium.

When the three officers arrived at the Catlett home, every female heart fluttered as David Southall entered the crowded parlor. With his sun-bleached blonde hair and deep blue eyes, David possessed more than physical good looks. He had Presence.

"I declare, I have never been in a room with so many lovely ladies. Including our charming hostess," David added with a deep bow to the pudgy Miss Millicent, who blushed and fluttered her fan at his compliment.

Smiling at David's triumphant entrance into Washington society, Philip glanced around the rooms only to find that the same people were always at these parties. Accepting a drink from a passing waiter, he leaned against the door jamb between the drawing room and the dining room, listening to a lively discussion on General Grant's resounding victory at Missionary Ridge in Tennessee. At last, the guests agreed, the North has something to celebrate.

Philip moved across the hall to the front parlor where two stolid-looking matrons were exchanging gossip about a young rake who was squiring an unnamed married lady about town.

"It's a scandal, Nellie," one lady avowed behind her fan. "Imagine, the nerve of those two coming here like that."

Nodding until the feathers on her bonnet danced, Nellie agreed. "I hear he is well connected at the War Department. The Secretary himself, I believe," she announced with pride, and gave her friend a knowing nod.

Smiling at their righteous indignation, Philip continued on through the crowd, looking for someone to engage in conversation when Wes Madison nearly knocked him over and spilled his drink. "Major, they are here."

"Who?" he asked, as he brushed the liquor off his sleeve.

"The one everyone is gossiping about. He's over there with his mistress."

Philip looked in the direction Wes indicated. He recognized the rake immediately, but a bow on the lady's bonnet obscured her face. When she turned to smile at one of the other officers, Philip's drink slipped from his hand and dropped onto the carpet without a sound. "Oh my God," he whispered.

His face flamed scarlet before changing to something dark and awful. He realized at once that they must have crashed the event, as Miss Millicent was far too considerate of Philip's feelings to have invited them.

As Philip watched the two of them through narrowed eyes, he reached for his side arm. With his fingers on the grip, he hesitated, glanced around at the unsuspecting crowd then shook his head. "Not now," he muttered.

"What is it?" Wes asked, looking concerned.

"Let's get the hell out of here."

"What about David?"

"He won't miss us." Claiming his cavalry hat from the maid, Philip stumbled outside, with a very confused Wes following behind.

After riding a few blocks at full gallop, Philip stopped in front of the Willard Hotel, still ignoring Wes' demands to know what had happened. Dismounting, he motioned for Wes to follow.

Inside the noisy bar filled to overflowing with soldiers, office seekers and spies, he downed a drink in one gulp before responding in a strangled voice to Wes' persistent questions. "The object of all this gossip is none other than my cousin Julian. The 'lady' in question is my dear wife Elizabeth."

Stunned, Wes leaned against the bar and mumbled, "I'm sorry. I had no idea."

"Damn them both," Philip swore, pounding his fist on the bar. "When I saw them, I wanted to shoot them both on the spot." He ground his teeth at the memory of Elizabeth's face, all smiles and sweetness, and ordered another double.

"Why didn't you call him out right then and there?" Wes asked.

"I started to, but I didn't want to bring scandal down upon the Catletts. Nor did I want the rest of Washington society to know my personal business. No, I will take care of them--when the time is right. In the time and place of my choosing," he finished in a voice so chilling that Wes shuddered.

"Don't do this to yourself, Philip." Wes tugged at Philip's arm. "Let's go."

Philip jerked his arm away. "Leave me alone. I plan to get good and drunk." Turning his back on his friend, he motioned to the bartender.

Wes shrugged and said, "As you wish. I will see you back at camp. Don't forget about the curfew."

Philip remained in the bar for hours, seething and muttering, "Damn the two of them to the very bottom pits of hell." And, he vowed to himself, I will never again let myself be blinded by another woman. As for that unholy pair, I will be patient and, when the time is right, I will get them both.

"Elizabeth, my love," Julian smirked, pulling on his yellow kid gloves, "you were the hit of the party. Thank you for a most amusing afternoon."

Sitting close to Julian in the cab, Elizabeth looked askance at him. "Why so smug, darling?"

"You mean you didn't see him?"

"See who?" she asked, as she flashed a saucy smile at a mounted officer passing by.

"Your ever-faithful husband, of course."

Stunned, Elizabeth slumped against the seat of the cab. "I didn't realize Philip was there."

"You should have seen the stupid look on his face when he saw us. It was worth a week's pay. Of course, being a gentleman, he made a discreet, if somewhat hasty, exit. Fortunately for us, he will never do anything to disgrace the Creighton name with a public scene."

She gripped his wrist. "I don't trust him, Julian. I have seen how he gets when he's angry."

Julian patted her hand. "Calm yourself, my dear. Philip may scowl at us but he won't do anything. Besides, he doesn't have the backbone, even if he got such a notion into his head. If he were a real man, he would have beaten you to within an inch of your larcenous life and thrown you into the street. So, you see, my dear, you needn't worry. We are both as safe as babes."

"You are a fool if you think so," Elizabeth said, stung by Julian's callous assessment of her character. "When he drinks, he becomes morose and is capable of the most vindictive acts. Please remember, he burned down my mansion just for spite."

Julian pulled her into his arms and whispered in her ear, "Don't worry, precious. Should he get violent, I will shoot him myself. What jury would convict me for defending your honor? Not to mention that you will then be a rich widow."

They both laughed at the happy prospect.

Chapter 26

FOLLOWING THE EPISODE at Miss Millicent's, Philip refused to talk with anyone or leave his tent, even for staff meetings or formation. Unkempt and unshaven, he rejected all attempts to bring him out of his depression. Wes Madison brought his meals to their tent but took each tray away untouched. At night, when he felt especially humiliated and hopeless, Philip stared long and hard at his pistol hanging from a peg on the tent's center post.

Two hellish weeks passed before Wes prevailed upon Philip to return to his duties full time. Feeling obliged to repay Wes for his kindness, he asked Robert to provide a pass so Wes could visit his family during the Christmas holidays.

Standing on the windy railway platform with tears in his eyes, Wes accepted the train ticket Philip pressed into his hands. "Thank you," Wes said simply.

"You told me several weeks ago," Philip said in a voice husky with emotion, "that you were unable to find lodgings here in Washington so that you and your family could be together at Christmas. I knew then that I had found the perfect way to repay your friendship and concern when I needed someone. Go home now and be happy with your family during the holidays."

"Nothing would give me more pleasure, my friend," Wes replied with a broad smile.

Philip watched as Wes jumped onto the moving train, the ache of his own emptiness returning to haunt him. For his part, going home for Christmas was not a consideration. Instead, he accepted Miss Millicent Catlett's invitation to join her and her brother for church services and dinner on Christmas Day.

In Epiphany Episcopal Church on fashionable G Street, Philip found himself caught up in the spirit of the season and joined in the singing of carols. During dinner at the Catletts' home, featuring turkey, dressing and oysters from Harvey's Oyster Bar, Miss Millicent's cousin, Miss Hallie, kept Philip amused with her firm opinions on current events.

Although she was not unpleasant to the eye, with her gray eyes and creamy complexion, she was the antithesis of the pudgy Miss Millicent with her slim figure. However, Philip found Miss Hallie's pronouncements about women's rights and the suffrage movement a bit off-putting.

"I am a staunch supporter of Elizabeth Cady Stanton and Susan B. Anthony," she informed him. "And a faithful reader of Godey's Ladies' Book. I have great admiration for the editor, Mrs. Sarah Hale."

Feigning interest, Philip winked with amusement at Congressman Catlett and his likewise unmarried male cousins across the table from him.

"Well," Miss Millicent said at the end of the hearty meal, daintily dabbing her napkin to her lips, "shall we retire to the parlor for more wassail? Afterward, I will play Christmas carols on the piano. Who would like to lead the singing?"

After an hour of listening to the Catlett cousins butcher the carols with their less than melodic voices, Philip set his cup of wassail aside and stood up. "Miss Millicent, I am reticent to leave this cozy fireside and such good company, but I must start back to our encampment."

"Before you go, I have a little something for you." She hurried away to the dining room. Bowing over Miss Hallie's hand, Philip thanked her for a most delightful afternoon.

"It has been an honor meeting you, Major Creighton," she murmured, and batted her pale lashes. "I do hope we will meet again."

"I look forward to that day, Miss Catlett." Suppressing a grin, he turned from the blushing maiden lady to his host. "Congressman Catlett, a happy Christmas to you, sir. And thank you for inviting me. It was a most pleasant day."

"We are delighted you could join us," the congressman said, glowing with good cheer and spiked wassail.

Philip bowed to the male Catlett cousins and wished them a happy Christmas before joining Miss Millicent in the front hall.

"Here you are, dear boy," she said, thrusting a neatly wrapped package into his hands. "I thought you might like some homemade holiday treats."

"How kind of you to fuss over me like this. You know, my dear," he added with a wry grin, "I have always considered you part mother-hen and part coquette. But after your thoughtfulness for including me in this family celebration, I believe you are mostly coquette. And a saucy one at that." He kissed her ample cheek.

"Oh my," she said, swooning and fluttering her hands, "I haven't been kissed by such a handsome young officer since Bob Lee and the boys went off to Mexico back in--well, anyway, it was a few years ago. Remember," she whispered, pressing his hand between hers, "our door is always open to you."

"I am grateful for your kindness, dear lady. Thank you." With her package under his arm, he gave her a smile before going out into the cold, the cape of his greatcoat fluttering in the wind.

Wes returned to Washington on that bitterly cold first day of January, 1864, looking rested and content. He and Philip decided to forego the annual New Year's Day reception at the White House. Instead, they huddled against the cold in their tent and ate the rum cake Jane had sent to Philip.

"How thoughtful," Philip said, eyeing the goodies. "I feel bad that I did not send her a gift."

"How can you say that?" Wes asked with raised eyebrows. "When I walked into the house unannounced, I thought Jane was going to faint. It was the best gift either of us could have had."

Philip regarded Wes intently. "I hope you realize what a lucky man you are."

Smiling, Wes lowered his gaze. "When I held Jane in my arms, I knew I had everything a man could wish for. My New Year's wish for you, Philip, is that you find the same happiness."

An uncomfortable silence fell over the tent before Philip cleared his throat and forced a smile. "Thank Jane for this delicious rum cake. No, on second thought, I will thank her myself. The least I can do is to write her a note."

They savored the cake while Wes regaled Philip with stories about how much his daughters had grown. "When it came time to leave," he continued, his voice suddenly faltering, "getting on the train was more difficult than the first time I left.

"I imagine it was. Now," Philip said, feeling the effects of the rum cake, "let me tell you about my Christmas. Miss Millicent and Congressman Catlett invited me to join them and several of their unmarried cousins for dinner. I swear," he observed as an aside, "I don't think anyone in that Catlett family ever marries. Anyway, their cousin Miss Hallie--a very strong-minded lady--lectured me on the suffrage movement and women's rights."

Wes shook his head. "The country will rue the day they let women have the vote."

"There is no likelihood that will ever happen," Philip assured him, and popped the last crumb of rum cake into his mouth.

Chapter 27

"DAMN THESE WINTER rains, the cold and mud," Philip complained to Wes during the middle of February. "I need to sleep on something that doesn't squish. I have decided to take a room in a hotel," he said, as he threw clothes and toilet articles into his travel bag. "I want a hot, well-prepared meal and clean, dry sheets for a change."

"After more than two years with no respite from the misery of camp life," Wes nodded, "I would say you deserve it. Also, while you are in town, you might look in on Robert. When I visited him at the hospital yesterday, he had taken a turn for the worse. Rachel is still there helping with the nursing duties."

"I'm sorry to hear that. I thought he seemed better when I visited him last week."

Wes shook his head with a doleful expression. "I'm afraid he's failing fast."

After a satisfying dinner in the hotel dining room that afternoon, Philip rode to the Armory Square Hospital where Robert was being treated for pneumonia. Upon entering, the myriad hospital odors assailed his senses. The nurses and the Sanitary Commission did their best to eliminate the smell but soiled bandages, body waste, and the rank smell of blood overpowered the strong soap used to scrub the floors and linens.

Walking between the rows of beds, Philip nodded to a soldier in a wheel chair, the stubs of his amputated legs barely reaching the end of the seat. Other men stared up at him from their cots, others saluted him. One group looked up from their card game long enough to note his passing.

As he approached Robert's cot, he saw Rachel kneeling on the floor beside him, sobbing pitifully. A quick glance at the sheet covering Robert's face explained her grief and he felt his heart sink. His friend, his link to the past and happier days, was gone. In that moment of personal loss, he realized that his life would never be the same.

But the smells of the hospital and the intensity of Rachel's grief jolted him back to reality. I must not dwell on that now, his logical voice nudged him. I must look to the issues at hand.

He bent and, gently helping Rachel to her feet, he whispered, "Rachel, dear, I am so sorry."

Grasping Philip's hands for support, she whimpered, "He's gone, Philip. My Robert is gone. What will I do without him?"

He took her into his arms. "When did it happen?"

"About a half hour ago. I could not bear to let them take him. Not yet. If I do..." She buried her face in Philip's shoulder.

"You must," he urged. "And I will do all I can to assist you. There are people to be notified and endless paper work."

"Please," she sobbed, "come back to Crossroads with me. I cannot do this alone."

Drawing her closer, he stared over her head at the sheet covering Robert's body. The thought of returning to Crossroads made him shudder with dread. But, he thought, what else can I do? Robert was my friend. How can I refuse Rachel in her hour of need?

A nurse tapped him on the shoulder and said with sympathy, "Major, I hesitate to intrude, but the corpsmen are here for Colonel Strickland's body. Unfortunately, we need the bed."

Responding to the urgency in the nurse's voice, he nodded. "Tell them to take him to Brown and Alexander for the embalming. We would like to leave tomorrow afternoon, if at all possible."

"Thank you, Philip," Rachel said through her tears. "It would mean so much to me."

"I cannot allow you to travel unescorted." he said. "And as I am already on furlough, I will ask to have it extended."

The bleak winter landscape slid past the train bearing the body of Robert Strickland. But all this was unseen by his grief-stricken widow and a reluctant Philip Creighton. As they drew near Crossroads, Philip's trepidation of returning home increased. Only something as pressing as my friend's death could have forced me back here, he thought. On the other hand, at least I won't have to worry about running into Elizabeth for the next few days.

In the bustling Crossroads depot, Philip waited beside the heavily-veiled Rachel as Robert's casket was unloaded. Looking around, he saw soldiers arriving home for furloughs, while others bid tearful farewells to family and friends. One-legged men leaned on crutches, while others had empty sleeves pinned up. Several wore patches to cover the loss of an eye.

As the train's whistle signaled its imminent departure, young girls cried and clung to their loved ones. Ladies waved handkerchiefs at anxious faces pressed against sooty train windows with one last look of longing.

Shaking his head at the bittersweet scene, he escorted Rachel through the jostling crowds and traffic, looking for his carriage. To his surprise, Elizabeth's driver, Ames, came forward out of the crowd.

"Welcome home, Mr. Creighton," he said with a formal bow. "Allow me to take your bag."

"Thank you, Ames. Where is Martin?"

"In bed with a cold, sir. This damp weather has only worsened his condition."

"The poor fellow. I hope he is better soon. Please take Mrs. Strickland's bag then drive us to her home. I will show you where it is."

Ames removed his hat and said to Rachel, "Allow me to offer my condolences, Mrs. Strickland."

"Thank you, Ames," she replied, and accepted his assistance into Philip's carriage.

As they passed Center Street, Philip looked toward the family mansion standing alone in the middle of the block behind ancient maple trees. His gaze wandered up the hill where the charred remains of what should have been his own home lay, neglected and forgotten. He turned away from the oppressive feelings the memories evoked and gave Rachel his full attention.

"I hate this war," Rachel cried into her handkerchief. "Is it wrong of me to feel this way?"

"Of course not," he assured her with a pat on her arm. "I feel the same way myself."

She turned toward him with a puzzled expression. "Why did you join the army?"

His mind drifted back to the abandoned ashes on the hill and his true motive for joining the army. "We all have our own reasons," he answered in a faraway voice.

After seeing Rachel home, Philip promised to return the next day then steeled himself to go to his own home, that place of dreaded memories.

The next afternoon, as Denton Cobb entered Philip's study, he was surprised by the warmth of Philip's greeting. "Thank you for coming on such short notice, Denton. It's good to see you again. I just wish the circumstances were different."

Denton's eyes misted. "I can't believe Robert is gone. I have already called upon Rachel and she seems to be bearing up better than I expected. It will be difficult and lonely for her, raising those two young boys alone. Well," he said, taking a seat before the fire, "what do you need? Your message sounded imperative." He removed and cleaned his spectacles on his kerchief while Philip paced back and forth, running an impatient hand through his hair.

Philip hesitated a moment before asking, "Would you be prepared to handle a divorce?"

"Divorce?" Denton stopped in mid-motion as he was replacing his spectacles.

"Don't look so shocked. This has been brewing for some time. Naturally, I would prefer that Elizabeth initiate the action, but I will do it myself if left with no choice."

"Do you want me to wait a reasonable length of time after notifying her of your intentions to see if she engages an attorney to contact me?"

"Yes. I will decide how to proceed from there. These are my terms for the divorce. Use my desk to make notes if you wish." Philip ticked off the items on his fingers after Denton seated himself behind the desk, "it is my intention to give her the house, the contents, and her jewelry. The allowance to run the house will remain intact because I do not wish to put the servants out of work. For reasons I do not wish to discuss, I will not settle any sum of money on her. Just make sure the current provisions in my will are iron-clad. Elizabeth inherits absolutely nothing from my estate. Everything else goes to my brother, Matthew. Is that clear?"

Stunned, Denton stopped writing and looked up at Philip over his spectacles. "Yes," he said in a hesitant voice but to himself he thought, No, I don't understand.

"Well," Philip said, and heaved a sigh of relief, "now that that's settled, let's have a drink before going to Rachel's for the wake."

Nodding, Denton accepted the glass from Philip as he studied the changes in his friend's appearance, noting a few gray hairs and the strange new hardness in his eyes.

The smell of flowers mixed with coffee and food overpowered Philip when he and Denton arrived at Rachel's home. Going straight to Robert's father, he offered his condolences.

"He didn't even have the honor of dying in battle," Mr. Strickland said in a quivering voice.

Mrs. Strickland remained inconsolable, while Grace Kirby, Rachel's mother, nodded distracted acknowledgments to the mourners. At Philip's touch, Mrs. Kirby clung to him.

"How is Rachel holding up?" Denton asked.

"Poorly," she said, looking from one man to the other. "She has gone upstairs for a few moments. She should be down shortly."

"We will wait in the dining room," Philip said.

Philip and Denton accepted coffee from one of Robert's cousins before sitting down to marvel at the changes in their lives. "There are just the three of us now--you, me and Leland Myles," Philip said with a sigh. "How many of us will be left at the end of this damned war?"

Before Denton could respond, Rachel approached them, her hands reaching for them. "How kind of you both to come and be with me."

Denton kissed her cheek. "Friends take care of one another, my dear."

"How are your boys doing?" Philip asked.

She shook her head. "Not very well. They are staying with a friend whose children are nine and ten years old, about the same ages as Robbie and Jamie. They want to attend their father's funeral tomorrow."

As Rachel said this, Philip glanced beyond her shoulder into the parlor. There he caught sight of his parents offering condolences to the Stricklands. A shiver of dread traveled up his spine. Steady, he reminded himself. I knew I would see them at some point.

Once Henry and Ursula had moved on to speak to the other mourners, Philip excused himself, went into the parlor and placed a tentative hand on Henry's shoulder. "Hello, Pa."

Henry turned at his touch. "Hello, son." Smiling, he shook Philip's hand. "What a surprise. I didn't realize you were here."

Ursula cried out at the sound of Philip's voice.

"Hello, Mother," Philip said. Realizing that all eyes were on them, he placed the merest hint of a kiss near her cheek.

"When did you arrive?" she asked. "Where--?"

"Have you spoken your condolences to Rachel?" he interrupted her obvious question.

"Not yet. Oh, here she is now. Rachel, my dear," Ursula said in her most consoling voice.

At that point, Henry pulled Philip aside. "When did you arrive?"

"Rachel and I arrived yesterday afternoon with Robert's body." At Henry's annoyed look, he hastened to add, "There has been so much to do, helping Rachel and all, I have not had the opportunity to call on you. And last night, I wanted to do nothing but sleep on something that wasn't a damp, sagging cot."

"I understand," Henry nodded, "but do you plan to visit with your own family?"

"I--I hadn't thought that far ahead. Events that affect everyone's future and the future of the Union are occurring in Washington so quickly that it is impossible to make plans."

Henry leaned closer and whispered tersely, "In light of that unpleasant possibility, and despite what has happened between you and your mother, I must insist. After all, you have the rest of us to consider."

Philip's gaze drifted to where Robert lay in repose and thought, Will I be next? Will I see any of my family again once the army begins its push toward Richmond?

"Very well," he nodded gravely, "I will come tomorrow evening after the funeral service."

"Good," Henry said. "Now, let's go back into the parlor and act like a family."

Chapter 28

SHORTLY AFTER SIX o'clock the next evening, Philip rang the bell at his parents' home then entered. It had been over two years since he last stood in this foyer.

"Philip," Jessica cried when she saw him, and threw herself into his arms. "You look wonderful. And, my, aren't you handsome in your uniform."

"Hello, little sister," he said, giving her a kiss. "Let me look at you. You certainly have grown into quite a young lady these past few years."

"How you do go on," she said, blushing. "Will you be with us long?"

"I can't really say," he said, his look now evasive. "At this point, nothing is certain."

"Oh, I'm disappointed," she pouted.

Just then, Ursula walked into the hall from the dining room. Mother and son regarded one another for several long moments down the length of the hall. Neither smiled nor made a move to speak.

Then, smoothing her hair, Ursula forced a smile and hesitated a second before walking toward him. "Good evening, Philip."

"Hello, Mother," he said in a formal tone. A familial sentiment tugged at his heart but he did not offer to kiss her or take her hand. He stared down at his cavalry boots then glanced beyond her to the kitchen. "I smell familiar aromas emanating from the kitchen. I have often dreamt of Gerta's homemade noodles and custard pies."

"I hope you will not be disappointed," she responded dryly. "Here is your father," she said as Henry walked out of the parlor. "We can go in now. George and Ellen are already here.

"Did I hear my name," George asked as the four of them entered the dining room.

"George," Philip said, embracing him. "You look great. Family life agrees with you."

"I suppose so," George admitted with an uncertain hitch of his shoulder. "Come in and say hello to Ellen and the children."

Wonderful, Philip thought with a groan, just what I have been looking forward to.

Ellen looked up from wrestling with her squirming children, her expression harried. "George, help me with Purvis. He is in such a foul mood. Hello, Philip. You're thin. Doesn't the army feed you?"

Swallowing the bile rising in his throat at her gracious greeting, he said, "Hello, Ellen." He bent over his nephew and extended his hand, "Hello, Purvis. I am your Uncle Philip."

Purvis studied him a moment before squalling at the top of his voice.

Unnerved, Philip turned his attention to the older child, Enid. "My, aren't you the picture of your mother," he said, marking the similarity of their long noses and pursed lips.

Ellen handed the children over to the nanny and asked with a smirk, "No children yet, Philip?"

"No," he answered curtly, and turned away from her. To Henry, he asked, "What do you hear from Matthew?"

At the awkward silence, Philip looked from his father to George, his expression fearful.

"Matthew has been wounded," Henry said softly as he took his seat at the head of the table.

Philip reached for the back of a chair to steady himself. "Dear Lord. How badly was he hurt? When did it happen?"

"About three weeks ago. Somewhere in Alabama. As I understand it, Matthew sustained burns when his artillery piece took a direct hit." Henry paused as he struggled with his emotions. "He telegraphed us when he arrived at a hospital in Washington. I will get the name for you before you leave."

"Thank you, Pa. I will look him up immediately upon my return."

Once everyone had taken their customary places at table, Philip said, "Tell me, Jessica, is Lieutenant Leland Myles still coming to call?"

Jessica blushed and ducked her head. "Who has been telling tales?"

"Lieutenant Myles made quite a fixture of himself on his last furlough," Ursula announced. "He seems quite taken with Jessica, and she appears rather fond of him. I cannot imagine why he hasn't spoken to your father yet."

"Let's not rush things, Mrs. Creighton," Henry said, his voice firm.

"Have you seen much action, Philip?" George asked.

"Being stuck in Washington all this time, the only action I have seen is escorting the President to and from the Old Soldiers Home, or guarding supply trains. Hopefully, General Grant will change all that when he arrives in Washington to accept his promotion to Lieutenant General. President Lincoln has great faith in Grant, and for good reason. He is methodical, tenacious, but more importantly, he knows how to win."

Henry pondered a moment before observing, "It is my belief that we would have won this war early on but for McClellan."

"I agree, Pa. McClellan is not much of a strategist or commander. But, to his credit, he did whip this rag-tag, bumbling gaggle of civilians into a disciplined fighting army. Other than that, he has not proven effective, especially at Antietam."

"Do we always have to talk about that awful war?" Ellen complained.

"Yes," Jessica chimed in. "Who cares about that boring old war anyway? Philip, have you met Kate Chase? I hear she is the most beautiful hostess in Washington."

"A time or two at parties," he replied without enthusiasm.

"What are the latest fashions?" Ellen interrupted.

"I really couldn't say. I don't pay much attention to that sort of thing."

The strained conversation continued until the family gathered in the parlor for coffee and brandy. After finishing the last of his coffee, George stood up and stretched. "It's getting late, Ellen. You must see to the children."

Philip saw a quick frown crease Ellen's brow. "Duty calls, doesn't it?" he said, suppressing a perverse grin.

She glared back at him. "Good night, Mother Creighton. It was a lovely dinner in spite of all the war talk," she added, shooting Philip a meaningful glance.

George shook Philip's hand. "I hope to see you again before you leave."

"That would be nice, but I am leaving in the morning."

After George and Ellen's departure, Philip stood before the fireplace and teased Jessica. "Well, little sister, how does Lieutenant Myles plan to support you after the war?"

Jessica pouted playfully. "We haven't talked about that yet. But his uncle plans to make him a full partner in the mercantile store. They even have plans to enlarge and carry all lines of merchandise so that one stop is all that is necessary for shopping. Isn't that clever?"

"Very," Philip agreed. "Do you mind if I smoke, Mother?" he asked, knowing full well that she did.

"Of course not," she responded through pursed lips.

"Leland has been nominated for membership in Father's lodge," Jessica continued with a smug smile. "It is an honor to belong. Isn't it, Father?"

Amused, Henry half-shrugged and shook his head.

"Only certain people are invited to join," she added with a jerk of the chin.

"What type of person is that?" Philip asked.

"Philip," Ursula chided, "you should be pleased that your sister may marry into the Myles family. Even if they are in commerce," she added with a disapproving sniff. "So far, all my children have married well. Which reminds me. I meant to ask earlier about Elizabeth but someone always interrupted me. Why didn't she accompany you?"

Taking a leisurely puff on his cheroot, Philip watched the smoke curl above his head. "She had a previous commitment," he said after a long pause.

Ursula gasped. "You left her alone in Washington with all those ruffians about?"

"She's not alone. I left her in Julian's perfectly capable hands."

"Well, if you say so. After all, Julian is family. Does he have a position in Washington?"

"In the War Department, I believe," Philip replied, taking note of Henry's subtle reaction when Julian's name was mentioned.

"I'll wager that my brother used his influence to secure a position for that rascal," Henry said, cocking an eyebrow at Philip.

"I wouldn't be surprised," Philip responded, taking his father's meaning.

"Have you met many interesting people?" Henry asked, changing the subject.

"Yes," Philip nodded with obvious relief. "The army is a cross-section of men from all over the country. The New Englanders are staunch Abolitionists and try to help the poor colored folks in and around Washington. The New York Fire Zouaves are always getting into some sort of mischief, but they have assisted the Washington Fire Department on several occasions. Personally, I find the mid-Westerners fascinating, with their strange accents and rustic ways."

"I suppose you meet all kinds," Ursula said in her self-righteous manner, "such as foreigners, Catholics and the like."

"Yes, I have. Take Lieutenant Southall, for example. What a roguish lady-killer he is. He carouses with the ladies on Saturday nights but never fails to show up for Mass on Sunday mornings. Our chaplain," Philip bent a significant gaze on her, "Father Brendan O'Boyle, has yet to chastise him for his escapades."

"You actually have Catholics in your company?" Ursula sputtered, and looked properly aghast. "And an Irish priest? Well, I hope you remember your upbringing and associate with the right kind of people."

He gave Henry a devilish wink. "Believe me, Mother, I am fully aware of everything you tried to teach me and am putting it to good use. Well," he added with a stifled yawn, "if everyone will excuse me, these past few days have left me exhausted. The funeral this afternoon was..." He paused and bit his lip, wondering how Rachel would cope with Robert's loss.

"Of course, son. We understand," Henry said, and walked out to the entry hall with him.

"By the way, I've written the name of Matt's hospital." Henry took the paper from the lamp table and handed it to Philip.

"Thank you, Pa." He slipped the paper into his breast pocket.

Jessica joined them in the foyer and studied Philip as he shrugged into his greatcoat. "I see a difference in you, Philip, but I'm not sure I like it. You mustn't let all those strange people change you."

As Philip buttoned his greatcoat, his eyes sparkling with mischief, he said, "If you detect a change in me, little sister, I assure you that it was not those 'strange people,' as you call them, who affected that transformation. Good night, all."

Chuckling to himself, he closed the front door behind him, leaving a bewildered Jessica to puzzle over his remark, and its application to those for whom it was intended.

Chapter 29

LOCATING THE THREE-STORY Wolfe Street Hospital wasn't difficult, with its four tall chimneys and the widow's walk overlooking the city. It was also apparent that, like many other structures in and around the capitol city, it had been a private residence before the war.

Upon inquiring inside, Philip was directed to the side yard where Matthew lounged in the shade, enjoying the early spring afternoon.

"Hello, Lieutenant Creighton," Philip said from behind Matthew's chair.

Standing slowly, Matthew turned toward him with a bright smile. "My God, Philip, is it really you? How did you find me?"

"Pa told me you had been wounded and where you were being treated."

Holding Matthew at arm's length, Philip studied his younger brother. The same guileless smile was there, the open honesty in his eyes. "You look good, Matt, although a bit on the skinny side. How are you getting along?"

"Mending nicely, thanks. It was mostly a concussion-type injury, affecting my hearing for a while, but my hands were burned." He held his heavily bandaged hands out for inspection.

"Looks awful. Has your hearing returned?"

"I heard you speaking behind me, didn't I? But enough about me. I see you have been promoted to Lieutenant Colonel," he said, indicating the new insignia on Philip's epaulets.

Philip sat on a bench beneath the shade tree. "Yes, and it was the damnedest thing. When I returned to Washington after Robert's funeral, I learned that the entire company had signed a letter requesting that I be appointed their new commander. Their confidence in my questionable ability to command was encouraging."

"Just a moment," Matt interrupted. "Did you say Robert's funeral? What happened to him?"

Sadness clouded Philip's eyes as he said, "He passed away late last week from pneumonia. I escorted Rachel home for his funeral."

"I'm so sorry to hear that. I always liked Robert. I will write Rachel a note of condolence."

"She would appreciate hearing from you. We were all saddened by his passing. Robert was a good friend. And it goes without saying that I would rather have been promoted for some other reason than this. I was surprised when headquarters notified me this morning that my promotion was confirmed so expeditiously, given all the activity surrounding General Grant's arrival."

"Congratulations," Matthew said with a smile. "You will do an excellent job."

Philip gave him a crooked grin. "That remains to be seen. Incidentally, headquarters also informed me that the Strickland Volunteers have been assigned to General Hancock's Second Corps as scouts and outriders."

Matthew cocked an eyebrow. "Hancock's Corps, hmm? Impressive. They have an excellent reputation." Then he frowned. "But I cannot believe you went home after all this time."

Philip's expression darkened. "Only my friendship with Robert, and Rachel's tearful pleas could have dragged me back there. Seeing poor Rachel so distraught, and her boys asking when their Papa would return, nearly tore my heart out. I had intended to slip in and out of town but when Pa saw me at Robert's wake, he insisted that I attend a family dinner."

Philip related the details of his experience at home--Ellen's shrewish comments, and his own pleasure at playing upon Ursula's bigotry and prejudices. He shook his head and added, "What I found disconcerting was that Jessica is becoming a product of Mother's influence."

"Pity Leland Myles if he marries Jessie," Matthew laughed.

"Heaven help him," Philip agreed. He leaned forward out of the shade, his expression serious. "Now it's my turn to ask the questions. What about the young lady from Virginia? Miss Hilling, is it? Are you still communicating with her?"

Matthew shifted uneasily in a straight-backed chair that had apparently been requisitioned from the family dining room. "Yes. Even though her father forbade me to see her long before I left college in March of sixty-one, we have been corresponding in secret since then."

"How serious is it?" Philip asked.

"If I could, I would marry her right now." Matthew made an exasperated gesture. "I don't know what to do, except to arrange a rendezvous with her, but no place seems safe these days."

"Why not ask her to come here to Washington? She could get a safe conduct pass. It's done all the time."

"Her father would never allow her to leave. Besides, even if she did come, I would insist that we get married right away. I know her father would never let her leave home for fear she would do just that. But it's more than just our ideological differences or the two armies at war between us. There is the difference of two worlds that can never be bridged." Matthew stared off into the distance, his eyes glistening.

"I'm sorry," Philip said softly. "Perhaps things will be different after the war and her father more amenable."

Matthew shook his head. "That will never happen."

"I wish I could do something. I hate seeing you like this."

"What about you? Don't you think it pains me to see how you've changed?"

Turning away from Matthew's intense gaze, Philip watched a nurse push an amputee in a wheelchair toward a group of wounded gathered on the front porch.

"I don't know what happened," Matt continued, "but shortly after your marriage, you changed somehow. Don't bother denying it, Philip."

"Leave it alone, Matt." Regretting his harsh tone, he said in a husky voice, "I'm sorry."

Matthew reached out to his brother. "You have been deeply hurt, haven't you?"

Philip stood up and, with his back to Matthew, said in a bitter voice, "I would prefer that we talk about something else."

"Things look different away from Crossroads, don't they?" Matthew asked after an extended silence."

Turning, Philip regarded him intently. "So, you have discovered that too." He returned to the bench under the tree. "Reassessing our values and changing our attitudes is a painful process, isn't it?"

"Yes, but it seems that you have endured more pain than I. I am willing to listen if you want to talk about it."

"Talk about it?" Philip twisted around on the bench, away from his brother. "I don't even want to think about her. The bitch!"

Matthew stared at him, wide-eyed. "Her?"

"Yes, Mrs. Philip Creighton, the toast of Crossroads society, and mistress to that poltroon, our dear cousin--Julian. Surprised?" Philip asked with a perverse smile.

"Astounded is more like it. How long has it been going on?"

"Since a few months after our marriage. They flaunt it openly now. I have been hard pressed not to run into them at these endless Washington society parties. If it hadn't been for Captain Wes Madison and Miss Millicent, I would have lost my mind by now."

Matthew shifted his gaze to an arriving ambulance wagon. "I'm sorry. I had no idea."

"Elizabeth put on quite an act to get at my money," Philip continued. "Hell, even Mother was fooled by her. You see, it was she who chose Elizabeth as my wife, and Elizabeth wanted my name and money. So our dear mother and Arthur Stockton secretly arranged everything, but only after Mother dispatched Samantha with lies about my intentions toward her. It worked out perfectly for them," he added, his tone resentful, "without a thought for me or what I had lost in the process."

"What are you going to do?" Matt asked, frowning.

He gave Matthew a smile that conveyed perverse satisfaction. "I've already done it. I have hit at the heart of what she and Julian want most--my money." Philip shifted to the edge of the bench. "You know as well as I do, Matt, that there is every possibility I will not survive this war." As soon as he spoke words, he realized that this same possibility existed for his brother.

"Before I left home in sixty-one," he went on, "I changed my will. I left the house and contents to Elizabeth. Everything else, the money, the properties, the bank stocks, the oil stocks, anything of value goes to you as my principal heir."

"No," Matthew protested by waving his bandaged hands before Philip, "I don't want it."

Philip grabbed Matthew's wrist in a desperate grip. "Don't be foolish. Who else can I leave it to? George? He doesn't have the brains God gave a flea, and I certainly don't want Ellen getting her grubby hands on anything. No, it must be you."

"No," Matthew groaned with a pained expression, "I don't want it."

"What are you saying, Matt? Is there something you're not telling me?"

Fighting to control himself, Matthew blew his nose before answering. "Prior to going away to college, I didn't realize how narrow our view of life had become at home. I had to reassess my values, as we discussed a few moments ago. I was glad I was the youngest son. I drifted along, not being noticed, and liking it that way. Mother never bothered to ask if I had a girl or was interested in anyone. No one seemed to care. No one, that is, except you."

After a moment of awkward silence, he said in a strangled voice, "Philip, I really don't want the inheritance. I want no ties to Crossroads."

"No, Matt, I'm not changing a thing. If something happens to me, you can sell out if you want. Give it all away, anything, so long as George and Ellen, or Elizabeth and Julian don't get their hands on it. Understood?" He squeezed Matthew's wrist to press his point.

Matthew gave him a reluctant nod. "Can we talk about something else?"

Philip sat back on the bench, leaning against the tree trunk and studying his brother. "Let's talk about my promotion party Saturday night. And you are hereby invited."

"When and where?" Matthew asked, brightening at the prospect of leaving the hospital. "I will even sneak out of here if I can't secure a pass."

Chapter 30

THE FIRST ORDER of business at Philip's promotion party for his staff, that happily included Matthew, was to offer a toast to Colonel Robert Strickland. "Hear, hear," the staff cried in unison, and raised their glasses in a private dining room of the National Hotel.

"Sir," Captain Peter Hanford spoke up, "if I may, I would also like to suggest that each of us contribute what he can for Mrs. Strickland."

"That's very astute of you, Captain, to catch us when we are all in our cups," Philip said, and withdrew two twenty dollar gold pieces from his pocket. "Collect the money and see that it gets to Mrs. Strickland." Dropping the money into his cavalry hat, he passed it on to Matthew.

"Yes, sir." Smiling, Peter Hanford accepted the gold coins and paper money.

Philip glanced around the table at this genial group of officers who so worked well together. Wes, who had become his closest friend in the company, and now promoted to Major, was a solid family man. Unspectacular in looks, with his dark hair and gray eyes, he found that Wes was trustworthy, an essential attribute in view of what they will soon be facing.

Wes' steadfastness and moral support had also earned Philip's gratitude during the dark days of his depression. Upon learning that Wes had been a textbook editor before the war, Philip warned that his editorial skills would be put to good use when it came time to write their After Action Reports.

At the moment, Wes was regaling Captain Hanford and Lieutenant Southall with the latest jokes making the rounds. A private tutor in civilian life, Peter Hanford was thin, fair-haired, had an infectious smile and a self-deprecating manner. He was also popular among the enlisted men and taught many of them to read and write. David Southall was the scamp of the company and a ladies man, but a good officer.

And then, Philip thought with a sigh, there is Lieutenant Jesse Hasselbeck who was recently assigned to the company. Not much of a horseman, or very talkative, he showed initiative and uncanny organizational skills. Tonight, Jesse sipped his beer, laughed at the bawdy stories, but contributed little to the conversation.

The anxiety of imminent deployment prompted the group to throw themselves into the spirit of the party by eating heartily and drinking a bit too much. With an uncertain future facing them, Philip leaned close to Matthew, lifted his glass and whispered, "To our brotherhood."

Matthew touched his glass to Philip's. "Our brotherhood."

At about ten o'clock, when the party broke up, Philip discovered that he had run out of cheroots. He excused himself from the group, saying he needed to buy several boxes in the hotel lobby. While standing at the tobacco counter, he was startled to hear his name spoken above the other voices in the lobby.

"Yes, Mrs. Creighton," the desk clerk was saying, "I will take care of that."

Philip glanced over his shoulder in time to see Elizabeth strolling toward the stairs. In a flash, it came to him--the revenge he had sought for so long. He hurried out to the street where Matthew and the other officers waited.

"Gentlemen, if you will excuse me, something has come up. I will see you back at camp."

Laughing raucously, Wes slapped him on the back. "By God, sir, whoever she is, she's a fast worker. But be careful, these camp followers leave a memorable mark on their customers."

With a wink, David told Philip to enjoy himself. The officers bid farewell to Matthew and wished him well, mounted their horses and rode away, singing about John Brown's moldering body at the top of their lungs.

Remaining behind for a private parting with Philip, Matthew gave him a questioning look.

"Elizabeth and Julian are in the hotel," Philip said.

Stepping closer, he studied Philip in the wash of the gaslight. "What are you going to do?"

Philip gave him a chilling smile.

"My God, don't do anything foolish."

"Don't worry about it." Realizing that this could be the last time he and Matthew would see one another for a while, Philip said in a voice now crackling with emotion, "I have enjoyed being with you again, but the evening flew by too quickly."

"I enjoyed it too. Thanks for inviting me." Then Matthew's eyes grew serious. "Do you think it would be possible for us to get together again before the army moves south?"

"I wouldn't count on it." Damn, he thought, how do I say good-bye to him? Should I spend this time with my brother instead of bothering with those two worthless wretches in the hotel?

"Well," Matthew was saying, "I had better head back. It's a long ride to Alexandria and I don't want to get caught by the night patrols with an expired pass."

Philip heaved a sigh. "I suppose this is farewell--for the present. Promise you'll write often, Matt. Let me know where you are."

"I will," Matthew nodded. "And you do the same."

Choking back his emotions, Philip took care in shaking Matthew's still-tender hand, now lightly bandaged for the occasion. "God bless you, brother. Take good care of yourself."

Matthew nodded and swiped away a tear.

They regarded one another for a long moment before sharing a silent, emotional embrace. Blinking back his own tears, Philip watched his brother ride out of sight. With trembling fingers, he lit one of the newly purchased cheroots and stood on the plank walk for a while, smoking, and letting the brisk night air clear his head.

Then, throwing the butt of the cheroot into the gutter, he turned and strode into the hotel lobby with an unsteady gait. Pounding his palm on the registration desk, he demanded with a feigned slur, "Mr. Julian Creighton invites me to his room for a drink but he neglects to give me his room number or a key. May you be of assistance, my good man?"

The desk clerk eyed Philip over the rim of his spectacles. "I feel it is my duty to inform you, Colonel, that Mr. Creighton has a guest this evening."

"I am fully cognizant of that. All three of us made plans to meet here. Come, come," Philip snapped his fingers, "hurry along, my good man."

Before reaching for the key, the clerk studied Philip a moment longer. "Mr. Creighton is in room two twenty-three at the back of the hall."

Philip bowed ceremoniously before sauntering off with a drunken swagger that bordered on the comical. After reaching the mezzanine, he ran up the stairs two at a time to the second floor.

At room 223, he put his ear to the door and listened. Hearing nothing, he turned the key in the lock and slipped into the dimly lit room.

Upon hearing the sounds of sexual pleasure, Philip knew he had timed it perfectly. He stood in the doorway for a moment, watching them in the faint lamp light, naked and groping each other. Julian was turned toward Elizabeth, with his back to the door. Elizabeth kept her eyes closed, abandoning herself to the ecstasy of the moment.

Philip moved closer and stood beside the bed. With a calm, sure hand, he drew his pistol from its holster, put it close to Julian's head and pulled back on the hammer.

At the sharp sound, Julian's head came up with a snap. Elizabeth opened her eyes, startled by his sudden movement. Beyond Julian's bare shoulder, she saw Philip--and the pistol--and screamed.

"I've got you, you son-of-a-bitch," Philip said through his teeth, and pressed the gun barrel behind Julian's left ear. "I can blow your damned head off."

"Oh, my God, Julian," Elizabeth wailed, drawing the blanket up to cover her quivering breasts, "he's been drinking. I told you how crazy he gets when he's drunk."

Turning slowly, Julian lowered himself onto the pillow, keeping his eyes fixed on the barrel of Philip's gun. "How in the hell did you get in here?"

"By giving the performance of my life," Philip said with a chilling smile, and dangled the key from his index finger. "As Elizabeth so astutely pointed out, I had been drinking earlier, so the desk clerk had no problem believing that I was indeed inebriated."

"What do you want?" Julian asked, inching away from the gun barrel.

"To begin with, the pleasure of seeing you grovel in your own sweat, and to show you how easily I could blow your head off. With the slightest squeeze of the trigger, like so," he leveled the gun between Julian's eyes, "you would be out of my life forever. And who would blame a wronged husband? Hell, if one of our own generals can shoot another man for seducing his wife and get away with it, so can I. I will do what the general did--claim temporary insanity and be hailed as a hero by husbands in three states for ridding the world of you."

"Goddamn it, Philip, you're out of your mind, coming in here and waving that gun around."

Before Philip could respond, a movement to his right caught his eye. Turning his head slightly, he saw someone in the shadows. He focused on the figure that resembled a maniacal drunk. The stranger's eyes, hard and determined, glared back at him from the mirror. Releasing the hammer on his pistol, he blinked, but the stranger remained.

My God, Philip thought in wonder, has hating these two brought me to this? He studied his image in the mirror a moment longer before turning back to his reason for being here.

Looking at Elizabeth, his stomach revolted at the sight of her. "I cannot believe that I once thought you were beautiful. Look at you now. You are repulsive, with your fat, pampered body. Like a blowzy fifty cent whore from Foggy Bottom."

"Please, Philip, don't hurt me," she whined, keeping her eye on the weapon he waved about so carelessly. "I will leave Washington. Never see Julian again. I will do anything, but please, don't hurt me."

"Are you begging, my dear? How refreshing. As for you, you worthless bastard," he shifted the gun back to Julian, "I came here with every intention of killing you but I have changed my mind. It has become quite clear to me that you two deserve each other."

Philip started to holster his pistol then hesitated. "Oh hell, I came here for a particular purpose, so I might as well do it." With a cold smile and perverse deliberation, he cocked the pistol, lowered it and fired between Julian's legs. Mattress stuffing flew everywhere.

Frozen with fear, Julian let out an involuntary cry and stared at the hole burned into the mattress so close to his manhood.

By this time, Elizabeth was cowering on the floor between the bed and the wall with her knees drawn up, hopelessly entangled in the sheet and sobbing into her hands. Julian, still pale and trembling, lay with his left arm resting across his eyes.

Philip holstered his pistol with a disgusted snort and stalked toward the door. Turning, he fixed a malevolent eye on them. "What's wrong, Julian?" he asked, looking pointedly at Julian's now-flaccid member. "You don't look nearly as piss-proud as you did a few moments ago."

Lifting his arm, Julian glared at Philip and uttered a profane curse upon him.

Ignoring Julian's condemnation, Philip snapped his fingers as though he had just recalled something significant. "By the way, Julian," he said, sounding quite pleased with himself, "when we scuffled on that eventful Independence Day four years ago, I warned you that I would repay your treachery. I believed at the time that shooting you was the appropriate revenge. As delightful as that prospect seemed, I see now that I was wrong.

"No, I needed to exact something much more painful than a bullet through your brain. But what could that be? Then it came to me, something that would be longer lasting and much more excruciating to each of you--like changing the terms of my will." He gave Julian a dark, mirthless smile. "And so I did, right after I walked out on you, my dear Elizabeth. If I am killed in the honorable service of my country, you will receive absolutely nothing from my estate. Not one penny."

Philip watched as the consequences of his words struck them both with more force than any bullet. Julian's ashen face blanched, his eyes narrowed with hate.

Elizabeth tried to scream in protest but could only manage to whimper, "No. Oh, no."

"Oh, yes," Philip whispered back to her with a satisfied smile. "Well," he said briskly, as though concluding a profitable business transaction, "now that we all understand each other, you may resume your previous activity. If you can," he added with a laugh before closing the door.

Chapter 31

ON MAY 3 and 4, 1864, the Army of the Potomac, 122,000 strong, crossed the Rapidan River at the Germanna and Ely crossings. Thus began the Union offensive against Richmond. However, the 66,000 Confederates, led by Generals Longstreet, Hill and Ewell, had other plans.

So, on a gloriously beautiful spring day, the two armies clashed at a God-forsaken portion of northern Virginia known as The Wilderness, with undergrowth so dense that it was impossible to see twenty yards ahead.

Many combat veterans vowed they had never seen such brutal hand to hand fighting. With artillery rounds, Minie balls and bullets tearing through the dry underbrush, fires erupted and spread rapidly. The cries of helpless wounded men being burned alive in the inferno filled the air. In the smoky, screaming melee, companies easily became separated. At one point, while picking his way through the smoke and confusion, Philip became frantic when he lost sight of his own men.

The action moved beyond The Wilderness to Spotsylvania Courthouse and, for five days, the two armies clashed in a series of battles that would become known as Bloody Angle.

After sustaining disastrous losses, General Robert E. Lee withdrew his weary troops and set up a strong defensive position along the swampy Totopotomoy Creek, with the Chickahominy River at his back. Determined as ever, General Ulysses S. Grant followed with his army, shifting around to flank Lee's right again

Moving eastward along the Union's left flank, the Strickland Volunteers, with no prior combat experience, were quickly forged into veterans. After being involved in heavy fighting at the Matadequin Creek, they continued eastward beyond Shady Grove and Armstrong's farm where at Old Church, they encountered Confederate cavalry.

Pulling his men back into the scrubby woods, Philip ordered them to dismount and consider their options. After studying their location on the map, Philip said, "If we split our forces, we can flank them, here and here," indicating the woods surrounding their location.

"Don't you think our position will be weakened if we do that?" Sergeant Powell questioned.

Philip removed his hat and mopped his face with his kerchief before answering, "I realize the experienced Confederate cavalry have a definite advantage over us but flanking them should negate that advantage. Major Madison, you take the right flank. I will take the left. Sergeant Powell, you come with me. When it's over, we will all meet south of here at this mill pond." He traced his index finger from their current location to the designated spot on the map.

Wes saluted. "Yes, sir. God go with you."

"With all of us," Philip replied, and swung into the saddle. Motioning to his column, they moved off at full gallop around the Confederate left.

Jabbing at their opponents from both sides, the Pennsylvanians gained a hotly contested advantage. While urging his portion of the company through a thicket, Philip's mare suddenly reared and lurched to her left. In the same instant, Philip felt a searing pain in his left leg. The horse stumbled and fell on her side, pinning Philip's left leg beneath her.

"Goddamn it, horse, move so I can get up," he swore at the animal that thrashed about in pain. Seeing that the poor beast was seriously wounded, Philip used his side arm to end her agony. "Sorry, old girl, but I can't bear to see you suffer any longer." He lay still for a moment, panting, and assessed his predicament.

Sergeant Powell had doubled back when he saw Philip and his horse go down and was at his side moments later. "Let me help you, sir."

"Thanks," Philip hissed in pain through his teeth. "I think my horse and I were struck by the same Minie ball. Had to shoot her," he groaned as he tugged to free himself. "Now I can't move."

"I'll try to ease the saddle up a bit, so you can pull free." He stood up and waved away several troopers racing back to help them. "Go back, men. I will take care of the Colonel. Go, while we have the rebs on the run."

Sergeant Powell turned back to Philip and bent to lift the saddle. "By God, sir, we might not be as seasoned as them Confederates but we gave them what for today. You can be mighty proud of the men."

"I'm damned proud of them," Philip answered, sweating profusely from the exertion.

Using his right leg for leverage, Philip tugged and wriggled as Sergeant Powell raised the saddle enough to relieve the dead horse's weight on him. Pulling free, he cried out as the ensuing pain set in.

Sergeant Powell crouched beside Philip and gingerly lifted his trouser leg. "Looks pretty bad, sir. I better get you to the surgeon right away. We'll ride double on my horse."

At the medical aid station several miles to the rear of the Union lines, Philip's wound was not considered life threatening, so he was left unattended on the ground outside the medical tent for several hours. He stared up through the dust-laden trees at the pale blue Virginia sky in a vain attempt to steel himself against the screams of the wounded whose shattered limbs were being amputated, and the low moans of those too far gone for medical help.

Near sundown, the company surgeon Dr. Franklin Cook finally examined Philip's wound. "It's a damned good thing for you that the Minie ball went through your leg without damaging the bone. If it hadn't, you would have to give up dancing."

Philip fell back on the cot, sickened by the sight of his own damaged flesh. "Just do what you have to," he grumped, "and save your damned sermons for someone else."

While suturing and dressing Philip's wound, Dr. Cook responded in his usual gruff manner, "Stop your damned complaining. I don't have to be here practicing genteel butchery in this ungodly heat, you know. I could be sleeping on my front porch back in Clarksburg."

"Yes, yes, I know," Philip sighed, and bit his lip to keep from crying out again.

Two days later, Wes arrived at the medical aid station adjacent to the busy supply depot on the York River. As he made his way toward the medical tent, corpsmen scurried past him bearing the wounded to waiting ships on the river. These medical transports carried them to Washington hospitals for further treatment and recuperation. Anchored alongside them, supply ships were unloading food and supplies for the vast, ever-moving Union army.

At one of the medical tents, Wes peered inside and called, "Colonel Creighton?"

Philip lifted his head from the pillow. Smiling, he waved Wes inside. "Come in, Major. It's good to see you."

"You too, sir. How are you getting along?"

"The leg hurts like hell, but I'll live. Say, what's that on your hand?"

Wes held up his right hand, wrapped in a bandage. "A bullet grazed my hand. Lucky for me I'm left handed or I would starve to death."

A look of relief crossed Philip's face. "I'm glad your wound isn't any worse now that you are in command. What about our men? Are they taken care of? Were there many wounded?"

Wes sat on a stool beside Philip's cot. "Just calm yourself, Colonel. Everything is under control. The company is doing just fine, and as the cavalry was not as involved as the infantry or the artillery, our losses were minimal, very few wounded. Those other poor devils, though, sustained heavy losses."

Philip winced. "My God, even this far away, it sounded awful."

"It was pure hell. Grant ordered a night march to Cold Harbor for the Second Corps. We were to act as support. They sent us a guide who took a short cut through this ungodly terrain. We stumbled around and backtracked all night. We finally had to cut our way out of the undergrowth. It took us fifteen hours to make a march that should have taken only nine hours.

"We arrived in time for the planned assault, weary and completely useless. But, apparently so were all the other troops and animals. As usual, confusion reigned supreme among the commanders. No one could get their attacks coordinated, so Grant was forced to call off the attack until the next day."

Philip rolled his eyes in disgust. "Nothing ever changes."

"The rebels, unfortunately, used that extra day to good advantage by building the most formidable defense works I have ever seen. It was an engineering marvel." Wes paused then said thoughtfully, "I remember just before dawn, I rode around a group of New Englanders who were pinning their names and addresses on the backs of their coats. They did it so calmly, with such matter-of-factness that it made my blood run cold. I asked a sergeant why they were doing that. He said these men had seen so much slaughter these past few weeks that they wanted to make sure the army could identify them and let their families know what happened to them and where. Good thing they did."

Shaking his head in wonder, Wes continued, "My God, Philip, it was a slaughter. Wave after wave of our men thrown against those fortifications. It was Fredericksburg all over again."

Philip leaned back with a discouraged sigh. "I do believe we have seen the elephant during this past month."

Wes' only response was a slight nod and a swipe of his left hand across his eyes.

Philip reached for his crutches. "I am about to smother in this damned tent. Help me outside and we'll see about getting something to eat."

"Good idea," Wes agreed, and helped Philip outside to a folding field chair. Once he was settled, Wes hurried off to the mess tent.

Presently, he returned with a private carrying a tray of cold beef sandwiches on thick bread, coffee, and a pitcher of fresh water. The two friends settled back to enjoy their lunch, and a brief respite from the recent horror.

After draining his tin coffee cup, Philip inquired, "What's happening now?"

"Not much," Wes shrugged. "General Grant wants the men to rest. I hear he is exchanging messages with General Lee to arrange cessation of hostilities so the dead and wounded can be moved from the field. Those poor devils are lying out there in this miserable sun, crying for help. It was the most pitiful sound I have ever heard."

Philip shuddered at the mental image. "What are the latest rumors flying around?"

Wes glanced around to make sure they were out of earshot. "I get the distinct impression that something big is in the air. I ran into Colonel Graves and he told me that Grant is already planning his next move. He wants to surprise Lee by pulling off something bold--and risky."

Wes took a sip of coffee then made a face. "Damn, we should force the Confederates to drink this foul concoction. That would end the war quickly enough. Where was I? Oh yes, apparently the General wants to move what's left of the army, over one hundred thousand strong, across the James River. And he wants it done in complete secrecy. He has already sent Colonel Comstock ahead to find the narrowest place for us to cross the river."

"What if Lee anticipates this move too?" Philip asked, shifting his position to get comfortable.

"Apparently," Wes grinned, "Grant has done some anticipating of his own. He ordered Sheridan's cavalry to ride west toward the Shenandoah Valley to destroy all the rail lines along the way. I hear Wade Hampton's and Fitzhugh Lee's cavalry are likewise on their way to engage them. That should divert Lee's attention long enough for us to cross."

"And stretch Lee's defense lines even further," Philip added with a knowing smile. "When does all this begin?"

"As I understand it, General Baldy Smith and his men are making their way by boat up the James River to City Point as we speak, with orders to initiate an assault on Petersburg. Grant wants to destroy all five of the rail lines that converge at Petersburg, which will cut off the food and supplies being shipped to Richmond. General Warren's Fifth Corps will cover our asses until we are safely across."

Grimacing again at the unpalatable coffee, Wes tossed the remains into the grass beside him. "Remember," he cautioned, "secrecy is of the utmost importance. No one, especially the press corps, is to know anything about this."

"Yes," Philip said, chuckling, "I have heard that General Grant dislikes reading the details of his battle plans in the newspapers before they can be put into action."

Chapter 32

AT DARK ON June 12, General Hancock's Second Corps quietly pulled back from their position at Cold Harbor. Heading further east toward Charles City Court House, Hancock then moved south and crossed the Chickahominy River before continuing toward the James.

The next day, marching toward the unknown, but sensing that something significant was in the air, high spirits returned to the troops. They questioned the reporters riding in the press corps wagon. "Any news yet?" "What's Grant up to now?" "What's the latest from headquarters?"

To each question, the reporters could only shrug their shoulders in helpless ignorance.

The Strickland Volunteers were assigned to guard the army's east flank, with Philip and Wes at the head of the column. "Damn, it's hot!" Wes complained. "I cannot decide which is worse, the infernal heat and humidity, or the dust." A swirl of dust stirred up by an adjacent supply wagon train settled over them, causing Wes to cough again. "I have decided," he rasped, "that it has to be this damned dust."

Yanking off his cavalry hat, Wes wiped the sweat from his face in the crook of his elbow. As he did so, he caught a glimpse of an incredible sight and called to Philip, "Look at those Massachusetts men over there."

Philip glanced off to his left. "They look like marching ghosts," he said in amazement.

The wagon trains, artillery pieces, not to mention the cavalry and infantry brigades stirred up the parched earth, creating a cloud of dust that enveloped the massive Union army. Already sweating profusely in their woolen uniforms from the 110-degree heat, the men were encrusted in their sweat and dust suits of armor. Compounding their misery, the overpowering stench from dead men and animals lying in the unforgiving sun made it nearly impossible to breathe.

"If we could only draw a clean breath," one man was heard to moan as he stumbled along.

Turning to make a comment to Philip, Wes' attention was drawn to something dark and sinister seeping through the dressing on Philip's leg. Edging his horse closer, he asked, "How's your leg, sir?"

"Still hurts like hell."

"Looks like it's bleeding again. You had better let Doc take a look the first chance you get."

"You are as fussy as Dr. Cook. It will be all right." Philip trotted off, ignoring his throbbing leg that was now encased in its own armor of hardened dust.

Initiating the brilliant sleight of hand conceived by General Grant, Union boats transported General Birney's division of the Second Corps from Wyanoke Neck to the south shore of the James River on the morning of June 14.

During the afternoon, General Benham's engineer brigade began work on a pontoon bridge. They worked their way from each shore toward the center of the river, a distance of 2,100 feet.

Under General Grant's watchful eye, the rest of the army crossed without major incident, except for a small boat that snagged the bridge and pulled several pontoons loose from their anchorage.

Taking their turn in orderly succession, the Strickland Volunteers boarded one of the transports late that night by the light of a full moon. Wes leaned on the ship's rail and watched the moonlight trailing in the ships' wake on the rippling water. "After marching around in this damned dust," he said with a smile of relief, "how refreshing it is to breathe this fresh open air."

"Yes," Philip nodded. "I'm sick of strangling on dust with every breath I take. Who would have guessed," he added, gazing out over the river with admiration, "that this massive army could move so efficiently. And Marse Robert has not yet detected our movements."

Joined by Captain Hanford and Lieutenants Southall and Hasselbeck, Philip and Wes watched with fascination as the rest of the army continued crossing the pontoon bridge. The officers returned the greetings of the surgeons and nurses steaming by on medical transports under the bright moon. Supply ships followed close behind in their moonlit wake.

"If our purpose for crossing the river was not so deadly," Captain Hanford observed with wide-eyed wonder, "this would seem like a festive occasion."

"Yes," Lieutenant Southall agreed, watching the activity on the river and both shores, "with all the colored lanterns the engineers strung across the river and with the military band playing, one would think those ships moving up-river were going to a picnic or a concert."

Their transport landed on the south shore below Windmill Point, near the field telegraph office that had been set up to maintain constant communication with headquarters. The Strickland Volunteers disembarked, claimed their mounts from below decks and spread out on the bluff above the river, joining the other cavalry units protecting the army as it crossed.

By five o'clock the next morning, the last of General Hancock's Corps completed the crossing and received the welcome news that General Ben Butler would provide rations for them. The Second Corps waited, but by nine o'clock, the much-needed food had not yet arrived. Disgruntled and starving, they began a frustrating trek, marching in circles and back-tracking in a vain attempt to locate a designated point on their map.

To his chagrin, General Hancock discovered that his map was inaccurate. Harrison's Creek, the position he sought, was miles behind Confederate lines. Hancock, frustrated by this latest confusion and delay, secured Negro guides and was finally able to march his men, suffering from hunger and the blistering heat, toward Petersburg.

With his leg still throbbing, Philip stood on the City Point Road, awaiting the promised provisions to feed his men. Suddenly, inexplicably, the ground became unsteady beneath his feet. It spun in one direction while his head spun in the other.

And then there was nothing.

Moments later, a soft black, whirring sound buzzed in Philip's ears as he struggled to open his eyes. His arms and legs felt strangely heavy and unnatural.

"Colonel! Colonel Creighton, are you all right?"

Is someone calling me? It's hard to tell with all the noise and confusion. Philip felt something cool and wet on his face, bringing welcome relief in this god-awful heat. Then a bone-rattling shiver passed through him, followed by a profusion of perspiration escaping from every pore on his body, further soaking his already damp uniform. He struggled to remove the cloth covering his face but his arms would not cooperate.

Dear God, he wondered, panic-stricken, have I been killed? If so, it doesn't hurt to die.

"Colonel? Can you hear me? Come on, men, let's get the Colonel under that tree."

Philip heard Wes' voice but it sounded so strange, as though he were miles away. Opening his eyes just a slit, he saw Wes' anxious face hovering over him. He licked his dry lips and asked in a whisper, "What happened? Were we attacked?"

"No, sir. Apparently, you were overcome by loss of blood and heat prostration. Dr. Cook is on his way to tend to you."

Embarrassed by his weakness before his men, Philip tried to sit up but the thumping in his leg and loss of body fluids had sapped his strength. Giving up in despair, he lay, embarrassed and inert, under the tree, awaiting Dr. Cook's arrival.

Moments later, the surgeon crouched beside Philip and rummaged through his medical bag. "Let's have a look at that leg." He cut away Philip's trouser leg then tore off the filthy wrappings with little regard for Philip's cry of pain. "My God, look at that smelly mess. It's already oozing green pus. Colonel, I warned you that it was too soon to discard your crutches or to ride. This damned leg will turn gangrenous if I don't get a poultice on it immediately."

Standing, Dr. Cook said to Wes, "Major, have someone bring water for the Colonel. He has gone about as far as he can today. We will put him up somewhere close by so he can recover himself."

Wes knelt beside Philip. "Doc is right, sir. After running in circles all day, with no rations and little water, none of us need to move any further. Besides, it will be dark in a few hours. We need to find a house nearby with a good well and lots of shade."

"I agree, Major," Philip said in a weary voice. "The men are worn down, and we cannot push these horses any further."

Forcing himself to sit upright, he braced himself against the tree trunk and looked to his waiting officers. "Captain Hanford, look down this road to the east. Lieutenant Southall, you ride in that direction." He indicated northeast.

"Yes, sir," the two officers said in unison, saluted, and spurred their weary mounts.

Ten minutes later, Captain Hanford returned, breathless, and drenched in sweat, his lathered horse wheezing. "Colonel, there is a plantation about a half mile down this road on the right. Sign at the gate says Howard Hill."

"Good," Philip said, and rose to his feet with Wes' assistance. "Hopefully, we can get the men something to eat there and allow these poor spent animals to rest. Dr. Cook, you can set up a medical aid station to ply your gruesome trade. With any luck at all, this exercise in futility will be over in a day or so."

Philip refused to be loaded onto an ambulance wagon like a sack of flour or, worse yet, like someone in need of medical attention. Still unsteady, he mounted his horse without help, grateful that the buzzing in his head had begun to subside.

Feigning more strength than he actually felt, Philip rode straight-backed at the head of the weary, bedraggled column that followed Captain Hanford to Howard Hill where water and rest awaited them.

THE END

Turn the page for a
sneak preview of

HOWARD HILL

Book Two in
Betty Larosa's 4-part
Creighton Family Saga.

Available soon online or
at local your bookstore.

'I am my beloved's and my beloved is mine.'

Solomon's Song of Songs
Chapter 6, Verse 3

CAROLINE
1864 - 1865

Chapter 1

SINCE ITS FOUNDING 153 years ago, the mistresses of Howard Hill had never given a thought to doing laundry--or any other menial task, for that matter. It had never been necessary before. That is, before Fort Sumter. Before the food shortages. Before the slaves ran off. Before the Yankees invaded Virginia.

Caroline Howard, current mistress of Howard Hill, straightened up and arched her aching back. Since early this hot June morning, she'd been bent over this washtub washing the bed sheets. Several times, she had felt light-headed in the murderous Tidewater Virginia heat, but managed to overcome it.

How delicious it would be, Caroline moaned to herself, to bathe my face in cool water, sit in the shade of the gazebo and rest my back. But there was no time for that. Cassie and Mina, the remaining house slaves, had already aired the mattresses and carried them upstairs. The sheets had to be taken in, ironed and put away after she finished washing the last of her undergarments.

Later that afternoon, while ironing the sheets at the back door to catch the cross breeze from the front door through the entry hall, Caroline cocked an anxious ear. "What is that commotion down on the main road?" she wondered aloud to Cassie who had just come downstairs.

"Don't know, Miz Caroline," Cassie said. "Me and Mina was wonderin' that ourselves. Sounds like the whole Confederate army down there."

"Haven't we had enough to deal with," Caroline grumped, and spit on the iron to test it.

As she folded the last of the sheets, Caroline heard her mother-in-law Dorothea call from the front porch, "Caroline, please come and tend to these people. They have no business on our property and are creating such a furor."

"How I hate this war," Caroline muttered to herself. "It can't end soon enough for me." Picking up the sheets, she started toward the porch.

At the front door, she gaped in disbelief at a sight she had never seen in her short lifetime living in the Tidewater area. A huge cloud of dust hovered above the main road nearly a quarter mile from the house. The cloud appeared to be moving toward the plantation. Within that awful disturbance, she could see animals and wagons.

As the mass of dust, animals and humanity moved closer up the driveway and spilled out into the meadow, she saw scores of soldiers--some on horseback, others in wagons or on foot covered with dust and sweat and blood, dropping to the ground from exhaustion and the deadly heat. But they are not our boys, she thought with panic. They are Yankees!

"Caroline, tell those Yankees they will have to move on," Dorothea Howard commanded with a wave of her fan at the intruders. "I cannot permit those people on the place while Morgan is off fighting for the Glorious Cause."

Caroline stared at Dorothea who rocked languidly in her wicker chair and watched the approaching blue-clad intruders through narrowed eyes. *Mother Howard truly is losing her mind if she expects me--a woman alone, armed only with freshly ironed sheets--to tell the Union army to move on.* She stood on the top step of the porch, one hand shading her eyes from the sun, and watched as a Union officer approached her on horseback.

"Good afternoon, ma'am. Major John Wesley Madison, at your service." Removing his hat with a gallant flourish, he bowed in the saddle to her. "In the name of the United States Army, we are hereby confiscating your property."

"What did you say?" she shouted back at him. "I cannot hear you above all this noise. Did you say you were confiscating our property? No, Major," Caroline shook her head, "I am afraid you will have to move somewhere else. We simply cannot allow Yankees on the place. Goodness, what would people think?"

"I am sorry about this, ma'am," Major Madison shouted back, his tone polite, "but we cannot concern ourselves with that. As you can see, we have many wounded who require immediate medical attention. And my men are exhausted."

At this point, an officer with a scruffy beard appeared out of the swirling dust and noise. "What is the problem here, Major?"

"Sir, I am having trouble convincing this lady that we are confiscating her property."

"I see." The Colonel fixed his intense black eyes on her. "What is your name, madam?"

She shrunk away from those eyes that were at once intimidating and pain-filled. "Mrs. Morgan Howard," she managed to say loud enough to be heard, before breaking into a fit of coughing from the dust. "I'm sorry. This is my mother-in-law, Mrs. Justin Howard."

The Colonel touched the brim of his hat to acknowledge Dorothea before turning back to Caroline. "Colonel Philip Creighton of the Strickland Pennsylvania Volunteers, at your service, and we are indeed confiscating your property."

"If you have come looking for food, Colonel, our own quartermaster department has already picked us clean. In case you haven't noticed," she added, pointing toward the empty fields in the distance, "we are in the midst of a drought. And now, you descend upon us like the plague and disturb the tranquility of our home with all this dirt and commotion, and expect me to greet you as welcome guests."

Colonel Creighton removed his dusty hat and slapped it several times against his thigh. "Madam, we are fully aware of the conditions hereabouts. We have been strangling on this damned dust for weeks.

But I promise you, we will be here just long enough to rest and feed the men and animals and be on our way."

Stiffening at the Colonel's course language, Caroline informed him in clipped tones, "In that case, Colonel, I must ask you to mind your language."

The colonel placed his hat over his heart and shouted, "My deepest apologies for my offensive language, Mrs. Howard. Allow me to assure you that no harm will come to you or your property during our brief stay. I will issue orders to that effect." After clapping his hat on his head, he barked over his shoulder, "Lieutenant Southall!"

"Sir?" Another officer rode forward and favored Caroline with a dazzling smile before looking to Colonel Creighton for orders.

At the handsome Yankee's smile, Caroline suddenly became aware of her distressed appearance and tried frantically to tuck in the loose hair that straggled about her face.

"Lieutenant," the Colonel was saying, "secure this area. Find water for the men and horses. There should be a well at the back of the house. And see if there is a stream nearby. Ask First Sergeant Powell to send a trooper up and down that main road to find someone who can tell us where our provisions are. Let headquarters know that we are encamped here for the time being.

"Then, after posting pickets and looking over the grounds, give me your recommendations at a staff meeting," the Colonel glanced at his pocket watch, "in about an hour. Meanwhile, I need to lie down. This damned leg is still killing me. I beg your pardon again, ma'am," he offered by way of a perfunctory apology to Caroline.

"Yes, sir." Lieutenant Southall saluted and rode off, calling for Sergeant Powell.

Caroline watched the Colonel dismount with a tightlipped grimace, and limp up the porch steps. As he passed by her, she wrinkled her nose at the odors emanating from his person and thought it had been a long time since he had come in contact with soap and water. Lowering her eyes to cover the awkward moment, she spied a bandage on his left leg spotted with fresh blood and wondered if he had recently been shot. This, she thought, could account for his foul mood.

At this point, Dorothea rose from her chair to confront the Yankee intruders. Her thin frame was clad in a blue flowered dress worn thin by years of washing and ironing, her gray hair pulled back into a severe knot. With blue eyes that showed no fear, she said with authority, "Sir, I cannot permit this invasion of my home. I must ask you to remove yourself and those--" she pointed her fan toward the front meadow, "--those ruffians with you."

Giving her a chilling smile that crinkled the dust on his face, Colonel Creighton bowed. "I appreciate your sentiments, madam. You have my word as a gentleman--"

Jerking her chin, Dorothea sniffed in disdain.

"--I repeat, as a gentleman, that I have already given assurances to the other lady that no harm will come to anyone on the premises. Nor will any of your property be molested. Now, if you ladies will excuse me, I must see to my men. After the staff meeting, you will be apprised of the rules to be observed during our stay, which I assure you again, will be of short duration."

"Rules? In my own home?" Dorothea waved her fan under the Colonel's nose. "I simply will not tolerate this. Caroline, tell this reprobate that we cannot abide such effrontery."

"Save your breath, Mrs. Howard," the Colonel said to Caroline. Reaching suddenly for the porch rail to support himself, he turned to the other officer, "Come with me into the house, Major. We will select a room best suited for my needs. And be away from all this noise."

"Yes, sir. Ladies." Major Madison bowed to Caroline and Dorothea before following Colonel Creighton into the house.

Caroline stood, as though rooted to the porch floor, and watched the two Yankee officers disappear into the entry hall, unmindful of the frantic activity all around her. Teamsters swore at the balking, weary mules pulling supply wagons, mounted cavalry pounded up the driveway toward the back of the house, officers shouted orders. But she was unaware of all this.

Yankees had invaded her home.

CPSIA information can be obtained
at www.ICGtesting.com
Printed in the USA
BVHW071933031118
532049BV00001B/52/P